THE TRIUMPH OF JULES COLETTI

BY

BRIAN FINKELSTEIN

FIRST DAY OFF PRESS

The Triumph of Jules Coletti

ISBN 979-8-218-83822-5 (paperback)
Also available in eBook edition

PROLOGUE

"Pass the salt."

"I seasoned the salmon."

"Needs more."

Silence.

"There's a new detective show."

"Okay."

"It's British."

"Sure."

"Or Icelandic, or something."

"But."

"What?"

"Never mind."

Silence.

"Fish is good."

"So good that you need to bathe it in salt?"

"For the love of—"

"Yeah."

Silence.

———

Night after night, decade after decade, this was the bulk of the conversation between Jules and Johnny Coletti.

CHAPTER 1

DECEMBER 17, 2016

FOR ONE REASON OR ANOTHER, Jules Coletti woke up. She was slumped on the couch in her baggy, forest-green Lands' End pajamas with her calloused feet resting on the coffee table next to an empty glass of white wine and half a bag of peanut M&M's. On the flat screen in front of her, a local Warrensburg, PA, reporter in a puffy coat stood knee-deep in a blizzard.

"It's really coming down now!" he yelled to the camera.

As Jules scowled at the weatherman, her eyes were pulled toward a little cartoon image of a different man. He was at the bottom of the screen, on a loop, turning toward the camera and pointing outward with that dumb smirk on his face. It was insidious.

Turn, point, smirk. Turn, point, smirk. Turn, point, smirk...

What had her granddaughter called those images? GIFs. Why did everything new have to sound so dumb? At any rate, his vulgar name blinked below his equally crude animated face.

Goddamnit.

It was still true. The man Jules had known all those years ago, the same piece of crap who was responsible for her best friend's overdose, had somehow been elected President of the United States. Her mind went down the all-too-familiar dead-end path she had gone down every night since the election. *How could this happen? How could so many people let this happen? How come no one stopped him?*

As was often the case, Jules dismissed the reality she was living in as too unbelievable. Surely, someone would do something. Help was on the way.

But who?

No.

No one is coming.

Enough was enough. Jules clicked the TV off, stood up with the caution and aches she'd become accustomed to, and tried to figure out how the hell she had ended up on the couch like that in the first place. She had no memory of drinking the wine or how she found herself watching the news when she started with a Christmas special. What made it worse was that the same morning, Jules had sworn to cut back on the drinking. She had good reasons to numb her pain, but she had been hitting the sauce pretty hard for the past several weeks. She knew she needed to rein herself in, and yet, fourteen hours later, there she was with a headache and another wasted night.

Tomorrow is another day.

She snickered at the absurdity of it all as she rinsed her glass in the kitchen, flipped off the lights, and made her way upstairs.

Normally, after washing up, Jules would read. Unlike her husband, Johnny, who devoured nonfiction before going to sleep, Jules preferred magazines. Sometimes, she would bypass reading altogether, turn the lamp off, close her eyes, and focus on her breathing to fall asleep. But she couldn't get herself to do either that night. Her mind was stuck on the news.

Screw it, she needed another glass of wine. Luckily, Jules had been around the sun enough times to know that drinking wasn't her disease. The nightly buzz was her medicine for the plague that was coming.

He is the disease, she thought.

An incurable sickness that, if left unchecked, will kill us all.

She planned to find an old movie, sink back into the couch, and reclaim her buzz to distract the racing thoughts. That idea went to pot when Jules glanced at the clock and saw it was 10:48 pm.

Dammit.

Johnny would be home soon. The only thing worse than feeling like crap alone would be feeling like that with her silent, but judgy husband standing over her. There was no doubt in Jules' mind that even though Johnny would be three sheets to the wind when he stumbled in, he would still make her feel bad about another empty bottle of Chardonnay—*hypocrite*.

Frozen, she stood in the kitchen sipping the wine. As much as she tried to clear her head, she couldn't get the GIF out of her mind. The grin on that dummy's face had sent shivers up her spine.

Someone should kill him.

Then, a thought deep down within her sprouted up—a thought she had been growing her entire adult life: *I should kill him.*

Jules believed that murdering the jackass would be justified. She also knew she'd be heralded as a hero by so many of her church friends for doing it.

What an idiotic thing to think about.

How could she manage it? For Jules, logistics always ruined fantasy.

Like flipping through the pages of the old Sears catalog, she saw ideas come and go as she ruled them out. I could run him over, but he probably never walks anywhere. I could hit him with a bat, but I'd probably break my hip just swinging the damn thing. I could stick a tarantula in his limo, except the idea of even getting close to a spider that big makes me want to pass out. I could hire someone to kill him, but where would I get the money? Plus, it's not like assassins advertise on Facebook.

She contemplated slipping him rat poison like in that old Dolly Parton movie, *9 to 5*, but where would she get it? Even if they sold rodent poison at Mickey's Hardware, how would Jules get anywhere near his food or water? All these ideas would be hard enough to carry out against a regular person, but now as President-Elect, he would have too much security. There was no way.

She went through the hurdles she would have to jump over to be one of those reporters, like in the show *The West Wing*. If she could finagle her way into the press pool and ask him questions as he got onto Marine One, then maybe she could shove him into the spinning blades of the giant helicopter. *Yeah, right, they're going to give credentials to a seventy-year-old grandmother with zero journalism experience.*

She liked the idea of an arrow going through his face and popping out the back of his head. But that made no sense. She couldn't shoot an arrow or ever get that close.

What if he fell into the bear pit at the Philadelphia Zoo?

Dumb idea on so many levels.

She laughed out loud at the thought of going to one of his stupid rallies with a bomb strapped to her body and just hurling herself at him.

Jules closed her eyes and felt her arms tighten around his neck as he lay sleeping in the Lincoln Bedroom, his vapid face staring up at her as she choked the life out of him. Then again, how the hell would she even get inside the place? Forgetting all the security and snipers on the roof, she couldn't even climb the escalator when it broke last month at the King of Prussia Mall. There was no way she could get over the White House fence. Frustrated that her pragmatic brain always ruined her ability to daydream, she gave up.

Whatever.

Just across Route 15 from the Colletti's home stood the Acorn Pub, a local dive where the top shelf was full of bottom-shelf booze. Camped out on his regular barstool, Johnny Coletti stared up at the football game highlights on the TV. Next to him, his two friends, Richie Devlin, and Ed Grigsby, yammered on about Roethlisberger's golden arm and the point spread, but Johnny couldn't give a rat's ass. His mind was elsewhere.

Johnny was thinking about Goodyear Tires. Even though he had worked there for thirty years, he had always felt the job was temporary. Throughout his career, he imagined that eventually, he'd fulfill his dream and find a way to make a living as a photographer. He never did crack that nut. Instead, he went to the tire store every day, stared at the clock, and tried to will the red second hand to move faster so he could go home to Jules. But since retiring and becoming bored shitless, that seemed insane to Johnny. He would have given anything to go into Goodyear and fix someone's alignment or upsell some guy in a suit who drove into Philly every day in an overpriced foreign car.

It struck Johnny as funny that he used to be eager to go home. He was so in love with Jules back then that being apart felt like torture. Yet that night, he was sitting in the bar trying to avoid his wife. He knew she was in pain, and he knew why, just like he had when it all started some five decades earlier. And just like all those years ago, Johnny knew he couldn't do a damn thing about it. Despite considering himself a creative thinker, he couldn't see a way out. Going home and seeing his wife was just a reminder of his inadequacy.

Johnny's thoughts of shame were disturbed when he heard, "Earth to Johnny. Bravo, Bravo, Kingfish. This is Delta leader!"

He looked over and saw Ed with his hands cupped as he mocked, shouting out their old Navy call.

Johnny flinched, spilling some of his untouched Rolling Rock as he did so. There was only one reason he put up with Ed: they'd done their basic training together. Richie, on the other hand, hadn't served in Vietnam, but he was good people. He was family.

Ed and Richie laughed.

"Screw you both."

Richie slapped Johnny on the back. "Where the hell were ya?"

"Was thinking about how when I was younger, I used to wish the time away. What an idiot I was," Johnny said. When he looked down, he saw that the spilled beer had soaked part of his flannel. He ignored it and took a steady sip from his mug.

"Was? You're still an idiot," Ed chimed in and laughed to himself.

Johnny acquiesced. "Probably right about that. I was also counting the hours until it's late enough to be sure Jules is asleep. That way, I can go home, away from you two assholes, and drink alone in front of my TV, which is the only thing that gives me any relief."

Johnny took another long pull of his beer and added, "And besides waiting until I'm sure my wife is asleep, I'm also counting down until the peacefulness of my death."

"And merry Christmas to you, too," said Richie.

The men laughed, and this time, Johnny chuckled with them. Christmas was in a week. That, at least, was something he looked forward to.

Johnny stood up. "And with that, I bid you adieu."

Ed looked over at Richie and said, "You're gonna leave me alone with the unmarried vegan over here?"

When Ed used air quotes to say "vegan," both Johnny and Richie knew that was Ed's way of insinuating something else altogether.

"Back off," said Johnny. It was one thing to joke around, but there was a line.

"Whatever. Take a look at my truck while you're out there," said Ed.

"Why would he do that?" asked Richie.

"Just thought you and he'd appreciate my new decal."

Johnny grimaced, downed his shot and then the rest of his beer, slipped his parka on, and stumbled into the cold winter night.

His boots made a crunching sound outside the bar as he stepped on the snow and meandered through the parking lot, passing Ed's and Richie's cars. It was really coming down, and their windshields were covered with ice. He was glad he hadn't brought his truck to the pub. Home was a quick walk away, even in this weather.

Before crossing Route 15, he stopped at the far end of the clearing to take a leak. He could've walked back to the bar or even waited five minutes until he got home, but pissing outside always felt better. It was one of the last joys left for an old man. Leaning against a telephone pole, he let out a large sigh of relief and tilted his head back to look up at the night sky. The endless beauty of the glowing stars and the sharp air brought a smile to Johnny's face. But when he lowered his head to zip up, he noticed something on the back windshield of Ed's old, rusted Suburban parked in the lot, which turned his smile into a wince. The decal Ed had told Johnny to look at was an image of the President-Elect. But what really caught Johnny's eye was the text under the picture: "Leviticus 18:22."

Jesus Christ, Ed.

Between flaunting his ignorance with the decal and his jab at Richie for not being married, Johnny had had it with his old friend. He had been a real prick the past few months.

No one was looking, but Johnny did that Italian hand-flick, under the chin, fuck-you thing, then crossed the desolate four-lane state highway toward home. There was nothing around for miles besides the Acorn Pub and Johnny's and Jules' modest home isolated in the rural woods. Johnny made his way through the darkness of an over-grown field, down a bike path, under a small, covered bridge, and up to the front door of his house, where he fumbled for his keys and went inside.

Jules was already in bed, and from what Johnny could tell, she was asleep. Still, he tried not to make a sound as he searched for a blanket in the hallway closet. Johnny needed one more thing: his M24 bolt-action sniper rifle. He preferred his Winchester Model 70, but it was upstairs, stashed behind the bedroom dresser. There was no way to retrieve it without waking his wife, so the M24 would have to do.

Back outside, Johnny spread the blanket on the ground and did his best to bend his seventy-two-year-old knees so that he could lie down on it.

Not as easy as it used to be.

As Johnny set up his shot, turning gauges and adjusting knobs, he no longer felt inebriated. Instead, he was focused. And in an instant, Johnny Coletti became definite.

After breathing in deeply, he lowered his head, closed both eyes, emptied his lungs, and slowly opened one eye to peer through the scope.

Inhale. Hold it.

He pulled the trigger.

Jules was about to doze off for the second time when she heard the gunshot outside.

Huh?

She jumped out of bed and walked over to the window. She could make out her husband lying on the ground down in the front yard with his old service rifle. He was silhouetted by the moonlight just enough for her to be able to see that he was laughing to himself.

What the hell is he doing?

It wasn't like she hadn't seen Johnny shoot before. He was, after all, a trained ex-military sniper. And their property in the middle of the woods was so isolated that he often placed targets by the tree line. But it was eleven at night, and he was probably buzzing like a bumble bee. It was weird to Jules that her normally by-the-book husband would do something so reckless.

He could kill someone.

And that's when it hit her.

We could kill someone.

She smiled.

Then she said it out loud, "We could kill the President."

CHAPTER 2

HOPING TO FINISH DUSTING THE hallway photos before church, Jules crept downstairs just as the rising sun snuck in. She'd tackle the pictures in the bedroom sometime after the holidays because no one coming for Christmas dinner—her daughter and her family, Richie, Ed, and Linda—would venture upstairs, but they would walk down that long hallway. Sure as hell, Linda would notice the dust caked on those frames. Ed's wife was always so condescending about the way Jules kept her home.

This from a woman who dressed like a female Columbo.

Jules had planned on asking Johnny to take out the extra ornaments so she could make the space more festive, but after last night, she thought better of it. There was only one thing she wanted to ask her husband now: to aid and abet in her murdering the President-elect. But she knew springing her crazy assassination plan on him would have to wait. The man was always so moody when he was hungover.

The black-and-white snapshots Johnny had taken—of farmhouses, cows, and trees—were easy, not only to dust, but to linger over. They stirred a quiet joy. But the portrait of Sheila, her college roommate, radiant at twenty, astride her 1965 Triumph motorcycle, pierced Jules every time. The way the young redhead had tossed her hair back after taking off her helmet and gazed at the camera captured Sheila's unparalleled ability to live life as if it were a contest she was determined to win. Ironically, Johnny had taken that photo just a few months before Sheila's tragic death.

Jules allowed herself a minute to wallow. Her mood soured again when she picked up the last picture in the hallway. It was a shot of her and Johnny's wedding; he was hoisting her up in the air, and she had her arms open wide as the sunlight from the stained-glass window in the courthouse shone on them. The fifty-year-old photo highlighted Johnny's utter bliss and virility, a stark contrast to her current, frail spouse.

Jules' trip down memory lane was cut short by the sound of her stomach growling. She stepped into the kitchen to silence her hunger just as her husband scooped soggy oatmeal into a bowl. His movements were sloppy, automatic, and abrasive. It reminded Jules of how men in prison movies would get their gruel dropped onto their trays. She cringed as Johnny shook too much cinnamon over it and sat down without looking at her. What happened to the man in that wedding picture? *There is nothing less attractive than watching this man eat. Who chews oatmeal?*

Jules poured herself a cup of coffee, finished the half-and-half, and dropped a piece of wheat bread in the toaster. Her mind drifted.

Last night, after seeing Johnny in the yard, Jules had considered questioning him. *What were you shooting at?* But she didn't get the chance because after he came in, Johnny sat downstairs watching the new Michael Connelly detective series on Netflix. So instead, she spent the next two hours staring at the ceiling as her mind raced, trying to come up with a "realistic" way she could get him to help her kill the man just elected President.

At first, Jules had felt anxious about not falling asleep, but then she remembered reading somewhere that puzzle-solving was an excellent way to exercise one's memory. The way Jules figured, planning the perfect murder would help her stave off Alzheimer's. Win-win.

But as hard as Jules tried, she could not fathom a course of action. The best she could do was assume that, since she knew the monster back in college, she could reach out to somebody somewhere and ask to get a message to him, and, given their history, he might even agree to a meeting. After that, Jules got stuck. No matter where they met, it would be inside. Using Johnny's skillset required her nemesis to be outside. There were so many logistical problems to solve.

The following morning, standing in the kitchen, she considered asking her husband to help not only execute her plan but also formulate one. After all, he hated the dummy as much as she did, and Johnny also knew that the creep was responsible for Sheila's death. If nothing else, Johnny was a great problem solver. But as she watched her husband at the refrigerator, shaking the empty half-and-half container, she thought better of it.

"Goddamnit!" he grumbled.

"Sorry. I just finished it."

"Then why put back the empty container in the fridge?"

Jules wanted to say, *the same reason you can't ever manage to close a drawer all the way.* Or *the same reason you misplace your keys three times a week.* Or *the same reason you have never once replaced a toilet paper roll.*

But all she said was, "I don't know."

"Jesus."

Maybe this isn't the best time to ask him if he has any ideas about how we could kill someone.

Johnny showered first and got dressed in his Sunday best—an old wool sports coat, a white button-down shirt, and brown Dickies—before he headed downstairs. And of course, even at church, he had to have that godawful, old Leatherman strapped to his belt. The man refused to carry a smartphone but always had his antiquated multi-tool just "in case." Jules put on her Macy's green sweater—would anyone notice the pilling?—charcoal slacks, and her most comfortable, gray orthopedic slip-ons. When she went outside, she found Johnny waiting in the Ford truck.

It hadn't yet heated up, so Jules warmed her hands by sitting on them while Johnny rubbed his together.

Finally, she asked the question she had brushed aside the night before.

"What were you shooting at last night?"

"Nothing."

"Nothing?"

"I saw some raccoons by the trash, and I was scaring 'em, is all."

Jules sighed. He was clearly hiding something, but she decided to back off again. They set off for St Joseph's Parish with scarcely a five-inch defrosted circle on the windshield to see out of.

As parishioners filed into the church's foyer, Johnny started toward the free coffee set up in the corner. *He should know better.*

"That's for after the service," said Jules.

"I want it now."

There was no stopping him. Jules watched, flustered, as he filled up a to-go cup and added a vengeful amount of half-and-half. As she turned to make her way into the nave, she almost walked smack into Johnny's buddy Ed and Ed's wife, Linda.

"Oh, good morning."

"How you doing?" said Ed, adding, "Where's that husband of yours?"

As if on cue, Johnny walked over.

"Speak of the devil."

Johnny ignored Ed and started chatting with Linda.

Jules caught Ed staring at Johnny, but then he turned to Jules. Something was up, but the service was about to start.

"Let's go, Johnny," said Jules.

"She likes to get in early to scout out a middle pew," Johnny replied, but not to her. To Linda.

"I hear that," said Linda.

As Johnny and Linda talked about pews, Ed grabbed Jules' shoulder and asked, "Did he tell you that he shot my truck last night?"

"What? No. He said something about raccoons in the trash." She knew Johnny was lying.

"Not unless one of those raccoons was sitting on my Suburban," barked Ed.

Jules looked at Johnny, who was obviously listening more to Ed than Linda, but he just shrugged.

Ed continued, "Oh, yeah. Last night, he got all philosophical about being retired or whatnot. And after Richie and I made a few harmless jokes, he went outside and shot a hole right through my bumper."

"Harmless my ass. And I was aiming for the rear window, but either way," said Johnny, joining Jules again.

"You're gonna buy me a new bumper, you piece of shit," barked Ed.

"Yeah. Fine."

"You could have killed someone."

God willing, thought Jules.

"God willing," said Johnny.

With that, Johnny nudged Ed out of his way, smiled at Linda, and walked into the nave.

Jules mimicked her husband's smile to Linda, who clearly noticed the pilling on Jules' sweater. Jules chose to ignore her and followed Johnny instead. Jules was too tired to deal with Linda and too annoyed to unpack whatever the hell was going on with her husband. Besides, she really did want to get a middle pew, and the service was about to start.

During the greetings, readings, prayers, and hymns, Jules began to drift. By the time Father Kuppler, a tiny, happy fella with a charming demeanor, made his way to the pulpit to deliver the homily, she was in a fog.

She had read somewhere that the President-Elect would be giving a speech in Philadelphia in late January. Since Philly was only an hour or so away, it seemed like the best place and time to kill the bastard.

The problem was that he would be sworn in by late January. Somehow, that detail made the deed seem more impossible to Jules. The security would probably be the same, and the task just as hard, but there was no way around it now: she was actually devising a plot to assassinate the President of the United States.

Goddamnit.

"Before we get caught up in the commercialization of Christ's birth next week, let us reflect on Philippians, chapter two, verse four. 'Not looking to your own interests but each of you to the interests of the others.'"

As much as Jules looked forward to Kuppler's sermons as a respite, she couldn't focus on him. Instead, her mind went back to plotting murder. The more Jules meditated on it, the more it became clear that getting her husband on board would be nearly impossible. She needed to pick her moment—a time and place where Johnny was relaxed and open to hearing new ideas.

Yeah, right.

As Kuppler droned on about the true meaning of Christmas, Jules rested her eyes, took a long breath, and fell asleep. Her stillness lasted a few minutes before Johnny bumped her arm. He was trying to reach into her purse to grab the half a bag of peanut M&Ms that was sticking out. She pushed his hand out of the way and snatched them for herself. Smiling, she shoved a few into her mouth and looked straight ahead. She could sense Johnny's frustration as he took the bag from her and accidentally spilled a few. The sound of M&Ms rolling around the church floor elicited a few head turns from the pews in front of them, but Jules pretended nothing had happened.

Meanwhile, Father Kuppler was still yapping, "Hopefully, we all possess the charity to give away food that we can't even find the room to eat."

Jules was embarrassed by these words.

Kuppler looked down, shook his head for effect, and ended his sermon by saying, "But I want to spotlight the charity of the David who stands up to the Goliath—the person who risks themselves to defend the other. And so, on this last Sunday of Advent, let us all find the hero we need. And let us all find the inner hero we sometimes need to be."

Jules felt inspired by these words.

I am the hero we all sometimes need.

When the time came for the eucharist, Jules' brain was humming. As parishioners inched down the left aisle, she was fixated on how to get Johnny to help her defeat her Goliath.

When they got to the altar rail, a middle-aged man winced with pain as he awkwardly knelt on the wood floor to receive communion, but his perfectly healthy-looking wife remained standing. Jules had to be thirty years older than the too-skinny-looking woman, and her joints ached every Sunday as she bent down, but Jules refused to not kneel. *It's disrespectful.*

"Take, eat. This is my body."

Jules looked up and saw Father Kuppler standing over her. She closed her eyes, opened her mouth, and received the wafer.

As she returned to her seat, she flashed the younger lady who refused to kneel some side-eye.

As the choir began to sing, "O come, O come, Emmanuel," Jules had an epiphany.

Christmas was the perfect time to tell Johnny about her plan. The man loved the holidays. *That's when I'll get him.*

She would wait until after Christmas dinner. It was still a week away, but nothing made Johnny more at ease than being around his daughter. Jules could wait a week. They'd have a nice meal, open a few gifts, and once Gina's family left, he'd be softened and more susceptible to an emotional argument.

Pleased with herself and her new plan, Jules' mind drifted to her daughter.

Jules had a tumultuous relationship with Gina, partly because she was jealous of Gina's success. Being an executive for a big pharmaceutical company afforded Gina the autonomy and sense of purpose that had escaped Jules. Gina's achievements only reminded Jules of her own wasted potential.

But it wasn't only Jules' envy that put a wedge between the two women. Jules suspected that Gina wanted something she had as well. In Jules' opinion, Gina felt left out of the bond she and Becca had formed. As much as Johnny and Gina got along, the connection between Jules and her granddaughter was deeper. They were like two peas in a pod. The two BFFs would see movies together and go out to eat, and, more often than Gina would like, Becca would crash at her grandparents' after she and Jules would stay up too late, overeating sweet treats and watching salacious police procedurals. Jules not-so secretly took pleasure in the way it affected Gina. *What's wrong with me? Why do I like making my own daughter mad?*

And the choir sang.

> *O come, Thou Dayspring, come and cheer*
> *Our spirits by Thine advent here*
> *Disperse the gloomy clouds of night*
> *And death's dark shadows put to flight*

Either way, Jules knew having family and friends around on Christmas would put Johnny in a good mood. If he were on board by New Year's, they would have enough time to shoot the President by the end of January.

At the altar, Father Kuppler made the sign of the cross and said, "Go in peace."

CHAPTER 3

JOHNNY SPENT MOST OF MONDAY bored out of his mind. In the warmer months, he could tinker around outside and find chores that needed doing. But it was cold, and there was so much snow and ice that he felt stuck on the couch, alternating between reading and napping.

Then again, it could be worse.

Later that evening, Jules used the previous night's leftovers to bake a ham and cheese concoction with some garlic string beans for dinner. She had been making that same casserole for years, and Johnny had hated eating it for years. The only thing he hated more than that ham and cheese was arguing with his wife, so he ate the damn thing without complaint.

Right as he was about to ask if there was any dessert, Jules' phone rang.

Who the hell is calling us at dinner?

Jules looked at her phone, probably equally annoyed as Johnny that someone was bothering them at that hour.

"Oh. It's Gina," was all Jules said before standing up and leaving the kitchen. "It must be important."

Through the door, Johnny listened to one side of the conversation.

"What? . . . What do you mean?! And Becca . . . She's okay? . . . Thank God, okay . . ."

Johnny figured it was teenage melodrama, maybe something to do with a boy.

Realizing he was alone, he looked for the banana bread he knew his wife had hidden a couple of days ago. He found it stashed in the hutch and helped himself to a generous slice. When Jules returned to the dining room, she looked at his plate and then up at him.

She stared at him for what felt like an hour.

Fine, I'll take the bait.

"Okay, what's going on?" he finally asked.

"Nazis."

"What?!"

"Nazis."

"I will need a little more information to understand what the hell you're talking about."

"Someone painted one of those Nazi things on the wall in Becca's school."

"A swastika? Jesus." So it wasn't boy trouble. Or not the kind of boy trouble he had envisioned.

Johnny started to cut into his banana bread.

"What are you doing?"

"What does it look like I'm doing?"

Couldn't she just let him eat his dessert in peace?

"I told Gina we would come over. Becca is very upset."

With that, Jules grabbed their coats from the front hall, handed him his, and headed out the door.

Evidently, they were going to Gina's. Johnny followed Jules to the truck, but not before slipping the banana bread into his coat pocket.

As they drove the seventeen-minute ride to Gina's house, Jules told Johnny what had happened.

"I guess Becca and Mia were on their way to class when they saw a crowd of students gathered by the science lab. When Mia walked over to see what the fuss was all about, she saw two giant swastikas spray-painted on the wall."

Like Jules, Johnny loved Becca's best friend, Mia. She didn't have the same academic focus as Becca, but she was kind, intelligent, and a bit goofy. As much as Johnny was proud of his granddaughter for being so focused and disciplined—she had already been accepted into Columbia University—he knew she sometimes struggled with social skills. Having someone like Mia, who was very popular and uber-social, in her life brought Becca out of her shell. Johnny knew more than most that being forced to grow up too soon limited one's perspective, and there was so much to do and see before choosing a life path. Being in the military—and combat specifically—taught him to appreciate the impermanence of youth.

When they got to the house, Gina ushered Jules upstairs to Becca's room, and Johnny went to find Carl.

He was not particularly fond of his son-in-law. It wasn't as if Johnny hated the man or anything, not the way he had hated so many of Gina's college boyfriends. Those guys were worthy of contempt, especially that one guy, Doug something or other. When that clown had been in the picture, Gina always seemed sad. Carl, at least, made Gina laugh.

It was just that Carl and Johnny had nothing in common. He was into elaborate fantasy board games and graphic novels—kid stuff. Carl was uninterested in reading history and clueless about anything topical other than entertainment news. Then again, Gina was also oblivious to what was going on in the world. Johnny, who read two newspapers a day, couldn't understand how his own intelligent daughter couldn't care less about current affairs.

But that wasn't the only thing that bothered Johnny about Carl. When Gina told her parents that she was marrying him, the first thing Johnny said was, "But the man can't even support himself." Gina made a good living, and Johnny was proud of her for that, but marrying a guy who worked part-time at a garden supply store seemed risky. Over the years, Carl started working more, but he still probably brought in only a third of what Gina made.

When Johnny complained to Jules about their future son-in-law, she said, "As long as they have enough money to feel secure, who cares who makes it?" Johnny considered this and thought that maybe Jules was right. Perhaps he was too old-fashioned.

But he also worried that Carl wasn't the kind of man who could protect his family. He wasn't tough. Jules had an answer to that one as well. "Why the hell does he need to be tough? It's not 1820. No bears or mountain lions are attacking anyone's camp. Besides, Gina is strong enough for both of them."

When Johnny found Carl out back on that cold December night, smoking a cigar, it must have been ten below freezing outside. Carl was standing there—looking ridiculous—in his way-too-puffy parka and Hogwarts beanie and scarf.

Man boy.

Carl gestured to the open cigar box without saying anything, and Johnny helped himself. Johnny had bought the cigars for Carl last Christmas and was happy to see him finally using them. They smoked in silence for a few minutes. Johnny was feeling charitable and figured he could try to comfort the guy.

"You know, when I was a kid," Johnny started, "a lot of boys in my school were into the German army stuff. Enamored more with the cool tanks and shiny uniforms than—"

"This isn't that."

"Ah."

"Apparently, there's a group of Proud Boys in Becca's class."

"Like those hipster Nazi punks I keep reading about?" asked Johnny.

"Yeah."

"Jesus."

"Yeah."

"This world." Johnny blew out a long cloud of smoke. "It's not like Warrensburg High School is the most diverse high school in the country to begin with . . ."

Johnny was pretty sure Mia was only one of ten black kids in the entire senior class.

"I can't imagine the conversations Mia and her parents are having tonight," said Johnny.

"Yeah. Or what about David Moskowitz, the father of the only two Jewish kids in the school," Carl said.

"Shit." Johnny didn't know this David person, but took a few minutes to contemplate how hard it must have been for him to talk to his kids about it.

"I don't know what to do," said Carl.

"Being with your family is exactly what you should be doing," Johnny replied,

"I just want her to be a little girl as long as possible. I mean, I know she's smart and not naïve, but she shouldn't have to . . ."

Johnny patted Carl on the back.

"I want to kill them," Carl said.

Wait. Was this Carl? *Maybe there's a backbone in there after all.*

"I know. I know."

Johnny continued smoking with Carl, letting the crisp winter air cool their rage.

———

On the ride back to their house, Johnny didn't try to start a conversation with Jules, and she didn't say a word either. He was enjoying the silence and the pieces of banana bread he had been breaking off in his pocket and secretly shoveling into his mouth. Delicious.

All was well until they stopped at a four-way intersection and Jules swung the pickup's door open and jumped out.

"What the holy hell?!" Johnny yelled at her.

He quickly pulled the car over, got out, and walked over to Jules. She was staring off at an empty field, her whole body shaking. It was so cold.

"It's going to be okay," he said in a feeble attempt to comfort her.

"How do you know that?" said Jules. She was livid.

He had no answer for her.

Jules kept going, "It's not going to be okay. This isn't just an isolated incident or a bad day. Something bigger is happening."

"Jules—" Johnny started to put his arm around his wife, but she pushed it away.

"Don't Jules me. Someone has to do something. Someone has to stop the piece of shit that did this!"

"I'm sure that the police have been notified and that the school will do something to punish this Proud Boy."

"I wasn't talking about him," Jules said.

Jules. Don't do this. He knew who she was talking about, but he also knew nothing could be done.

"Somebody needs to kill him."

Oh, for the love of . . .

CHAPTER 4

BRIGHT AND EARLY ON CHRISTMAS morning, Jules made herself some coffee and got to cooking. She started with the gravy, browning the sausage in olive oil, frying up some thinly sliced garlic, and adding the paste, water, tomato sauce, and then two big cans of crushed tomatoes. She threw in some freshly chopped basil, red pepper, salt, and a teaspoon of sugar to cut the acid. Next, Jules made the meatballs: a pound of beef, a pound of veal, two eggs, six pieces of white bread soaked in whole milk, a half cup of grated Locatelli cheese, some garlic powder, and parsley. She rolled them up, fried them in vegetable oil, and let them dry on a paper towel-lined Santa Claus plate.

Once the meatballs and gravy were done, Jules added a little Baileys to her coffee, found some Christmas music on the Tivoli, sat, and took a long, slow sip. The Baileys felt good.

By noon, the kitchen looked like an Italian restaurant. There was lasagna and eggplant parm, and Jules was just about done setting up a charcuterie board full of capocollo, prosciutto, genoa salami, pepperoni, provolone, mozzarella, gorgonzola, sliced tomatoes, and a mound of olives. She had also switched to Chardonnay and was half a bottle in.

She was still mad at herself for her impatience. *How could I just blurt out to Johnny that I wanted to kill the President!? Ugh.* Neither had mentioned it since that night at Gina's house, and Jules hoped he had forgotten all about it. Either way, she told herself, today was still the best time. Her husband would be eased by having family around, and it would be the right time to bring up the subject again. Onward and upward.

Jules was busy covering the deli tray with Saran wrap when Gina walked into the kitchen and startled her.

"Merry Christmas."

Jules jumped. "Goddamnit."

"Sorry. We rang, but no one answered."

Behind Gina were Carl, Charlie, and Becca.

"I can't hear anything, and your dad is out back with Uncle Richie," said Jules.

As she wiped some sweat from her brow, Charlie kissed her on the cheek.

"Hey, Grandma. Merry Christmas."

"How's my college guy doing?"

Charlie shrugged, muttered, "Chill," and then just smiled.

Oh well, good talk.

Jules clocked Gina as she walked to the counter, surveyed the food, and then judgmentally held up the half-empty bottle of wine to her husband.

"Mom. I wish you'd let me bring some dinner instead of doing all this by yourself."

"Shush. I like doing it."

"Good. Because I like doing this," said Carl as he grabbed a sugar cookie off a tray of sprinkled holiday shapes and shoved it into his mouth.

This made Jules feel good. Unlike Johnny, she liked Carl. She didn't pretend to understand her daughter, but she knew Carl made her happy. Jules wasn't even sure that was possible until he came along.

"Well then, at least let us set the table," Gina said.

"Okay, but we can't eat until Linda and Ed get here."

Gina and Carl exchanged a look. Jules knew they did not like Ed and Linda. Not that she liked Ed much either. He was a close-minded, hateful man. But what could they do? He had been Johnny's friend since basic training. Linda wasn't bad, though—a little ignorant but sweet.

Jules turned to Becca and gave her granddaughter a big bear hug.

"How are you, honey?"

"I'm okay," said Becca.

Becca reached into her bag and pulled out a tripod.

"What's that?" asked Jules.

"It's for my phone. I was hoping we could film that thing for my school that I texted you about."

"Maybe we can do that after we eat."

Becca kept setting up her tripod on the table. "Or we could do it now?"

Jules respected Becca's tenacity.

Becca turned to her mom. "Can you keep Charlie and Dad out of here while we do this?"

"Yes, sunshine," said Gina. Turning to her husband, she ordered, "You heard her. Out."

Carl looked at Charlie and gestured at the plate of cookies. Charlie picked up the plate and handed it to Carl.

"I'm gonna go outside and say hi to Pappi and Uncle Richie," said Charlie.

"Good idea," said Jules.

Gina grabbed a stack of clean plates, and then she and Carl followed their son out of the kitchen.

Once they were all out of the room, Jules sat at the table and watched Becca adjust her iPhone. "So, what is this for again?"

"It's for my Gender Roles in Modern History class."

"Education is a goddamn scam."

"Grandma!"

"Okay. I'll play nice."

"Thank you. We're studying the sixties right now. Just look into the phone's camera."

Jules looked at the phone and made a face. Becca pouted.

"Fine," said Jules.

"Can you say your name and age?"

"Jules Coletti. And I am seventy years old."

"Thanks. So why don't you just say what the 1960s were like for you?"

"Well . . ." She took a full sip of wine. "I kind of missed them. They didn't really happen for me."

"I don't understand. You were in your early twenties."

"Yes. True. But I was pregnant in late '68 when the world started to change. All that good stuff, like the music, sexual revolution, ERA, and civil rights protests, passed me by. I was more a kid of the early '60s and late '50s."

"What do you mean by that?"

"It was different for women like me back then. My world was all Elvis and Catholicism. What I mean by that is that I know you read about the free love and marches in school, but for me, it was different."

"Okay, Boomer," said Becca.

"What?"

"Forget it."

Jules took a few seconds to think about what she wanted to say, curling her lip as she did so. "Look, I don't blame your grandpa. At the time, even with most of our friends, the ladies didn't work. But I always had my career."

"Your dentist job?"

"Yeah. I was an assistant for Dr. Klein for over forty years."

"And that wasn't that common?"

"Oh no. And your grandpa always supported that. He was a good man who helped with the housework and did the dishes. In our group of friends, that was unheard of. Men sat at the table, and women cooked, cleaned, and cared for the kids. Johnny was never like that. This equality may seem normal now, but I assure you, it was not then."

"That's nice."

"It was. But . . ."

Jules got up and grabbed the wine. She sat back down, emptied the bottle into her glass, and took a long sip. "But old-world nonsense lingers, even for him. Every decision was his. I mean—" She paused to look at the food on the counter. "He grew up with Italian food at Christmas. My people had turkey."

"I like turkey."

"But it was like that with everything: where your mom went to school, vacations we went on, always with the sandwiches at Rocco's when I wanted to go to Soup House. The man hates soup. Who the hell hates soup?!"

"I like turkey, and I like soup."

"Every rational person in the history of humanity likes soup. Not to complain, but he also picks all the dumb shows we watch on TV and the movies we see. I wanted a dog, but he's allergic. I wanted a four-door, and he bought a pickup. I wanted to name your mother Gail, and he chose Gina."

"Gail!?"

Jules shrugged.

"Well, that sucks, Grandma. But why not tell him? Maybe he'd change?"

"Old dogs and new tricks. Besides, it's also somewhat my fault for letting it happen for so long."

"Okay. But if you told Pappi that you wanted to go to Soup House and get some lobster bisque, I'm sure he would be cool with it."

"Maybe . . ." Jules said as she started to stand up. "Is that it?"

"Last thing. Describe your sixties college experience in one word."

Jules wanted to say that she loved it at first. Even though she went to school just a few hours from where she grew up, it felt like being on another planet. It was so close to Philly, and it all felt so cosmopolitan. And then the darkness came.

Instead, Jules took another sip of wine and said, "Fine. It was fine."

NOVEMBER 1, 1968

Twenty-one-year-old Jules stood in line with the other college students waiting to get their tests back. She listened as her Economics Professor sat at his one-hundred-year-old oak desk, scolding a fellow student.

"What are you going to do about it?"

"What?"

"I said, what are you going to do about it? You received your second straight "D" in my class. I know you think I'm a demanding teacher, but that's not going to change. So, again, I ask, what are you going to do about it?"

"Um, work harder?"

"Good answer. I don't imagine you could work any less."

As the deflated student slinked away, the professor continued to call out names and hold their graded tests up for them. One by one, the privileged young adults looked at their "Cs" and "Ds" and then sulked out of the room. Everyone else waiting looked anxious every time they overheard their professor tear down one of their classmates, but Jules was unaffected. She had a unique confidence, and, as she found out when she saw her "A," her confidence was well-earned.

"Nice work, Ms. Dayitch. You have a bright future ahead of you."

"Thank you!"

Jules was elated but knew better than to engage her professor any further. She left the usually daunting classroom feeling like she could take on the world.

When Jules finally made it across campus to the koi pond, she found her roommate waiting; her red hair and perpetual smile were even brighter in the direct sunlight. No one made Jules happier than Sheila Newman, yet the two could not be more different. While Jules had plans to get her MBA, start her own business, and—in her own words—take over the world, Sheila's only reason for going to college was to meet a good man and get married. Sheila's plans, or lack thereof, confused Jules since Sheila was a passionate, multi-talented, straight-A student who could pretty much do anything she wanted to do. To Jules, having a career and avoiding self-identifying solely as a wife were the only reasons to go to college in the first place, to escape being average. But while the two ladies may have differed in their life goals, they were united in their limitless joy and wonder.

The roommates hugged. "Well. How did you do?"

"I got an A!"

"Of course you did," said Sheila.

"I want to celebrate. Let's go to Philly tonight. We can have drinks at La Conversation. My treat!" said Jules.

For as long as they had known each other, Sheila had always paid for things. Her family was wealthy, and money didn't matter to her. But Jules had been saving up for months and was proud to offer to treat for once.

"Oh, man. I wish I could, but..."

Sheila looked embarrassed to say more. Jules finished her thought for her.

"But you have a date with the Dummy."

"Yes."

Jules groaned.

"Not everyone is as lucky as you and Johnny. You two are a fluke. I'm pretty sure he's the last honorable man left in the entire state of Pennsylvania," said Sheila.

Jules smiled. She had known Johnny most of her life, but never actually talked to him until their junior year of high school. Jules was an active and outgoing teen, and Johnny was more of a quiet kid who kept to himself. Not that she hadn't heard rumors about his family. Everyone in Warrensburg knew the old man was an angry guy not to be messed with. And even though Jules suspected her parents would be happier if they never had her, she knew she had it good compared to what she had heard about Johnny's home life.

By the time they were juniors in high school, Jules was a member of the Honor Society, Student Council, and the captain of the hockey team. When she also decided to take on the Yearbook Committee, she got to know Johnny for the first time.

In the art room, one autumn day after school, he crept in and said hello. He wanted to show her some photos, and she could immediately tell that approaching her about joining Yearbook was a big deal for him. Jules was nothing if not kind and agreed to look at his pictures. When she opened his portfolio, Jules saw gorgeous images of trees, birds, flowers, and butterflies. There was also one stunning portrait of his mother that knocked Jules out. She was sitting cross-legged on a wooden bench at a pizza parlor in the Bronx. Her hair was in a classic beehive, and she wore a comfortable-looking sleeveless dress. Her dimples pushed her freckles up high on her cheeks, and her head tilted slightly to the left. Her smile was big and bright, but the ambiguity of her eyes floored Jules. There was a twinkle, a spark of joy. But she was also pleading for help. She looked simultaneously in love with the lens—or rather her son behind it—and miserable with her existence.

Jules looked at the photo for five minutes before looking up at the person who had taken it. How could a guy who lived in constant turmoil be capable of such beauty? Jules had been hoping that a boy named Tim Decker would ask her to homecoming, but he never did. But by the time Johnny asked her, she was all in.

"I am pretty lucky," Jules said to Sheila.

"You are. The way he looks at you and how you look at him. You two are like Lara and Dr. Zhivago. That's special."

"Ew."

"Trust me. I want that too. It just hasn't happened yet for me. And for now, the Dummy treats me nicely. And he's fun."

Jules made a noise that sounded like a cross between a moan and a squeaky door. Sheila understood that Jules didn't like her boyfriend. Jules had called him arrogant and had said many times that he wasn't even half as intelligent as Sheila. She suspected it was a matter of time before Sheila dumped him.

"Okay," said Jules with a look of disappointment.

"You should go anyway."

"By myself? I don't know."

"Take a book to read. Drinking wine in a café by yourself while getting lost in a novel sounds very chic to me!"

While Jules thought about it, Sheila hummed the theme from *Dr. Zhivago* ("Lara's Theme"), and Jules couldn't help but laugh.

After Sheila darted off to another class, Jules took her friend's advice. She grabbed a city bus and sat at a table in La Conversation, reading *Franny and Zooey* while enjoying a glass of champagne and a bowl of moules frites. Given her small-town background and her parents' limited travels, being in Philly by herself felt like being in Europe. As she sat there, she truly believed that her possibilities were limitless. Great things for Jules Dayitch were inevitable, or so she thought.

By the time Jules returned to the university, just a little after eight, she felt invincible. But when she opened her dorm room door and saw Sheila curled up in the fetal position on her bed, she knew something was horribly wrong. Jules dropped her bag and ran over to the bed.

"What happened?"

Sheila was too upset to say anything. She had been crying, and as Jules looked around to find some evidence of what had caused her friend's despair, the front door creaked open.

"Oh man, your bathrooms are a lot nicer than ours—" he stopped mid-sentence when he noticed Jules.

"Oh. Heyya Jules."

"What happened here?" asked Jules, this time with anger in her voice.

"Whoa. No reason to get yourself all worked up. Believe me, Sheila and I just had a great date. And I was about to say goodnight."

When he bent to kiss Sheila on her forehead, she froze, petrified. He straightened up, smoothed out his wrinkled shirt, winked at Jules, and left the room.

CHAPTER 5

DECEMBER 25, 2016.

BY DUSK, DINNER WAS JUST about done, but the holiday raged on. Johnny couldn't be happier as the Christmas music played, decorations hung, and the fireplace blazed. Plates were left dirty at the table, pants were unbuttoned, the wine flowed, and, as usual, Ed and Linda were holding court.

Ed stood up, flailing his arms around to tell his story. "So, the waiter says, 'You guys done?' And I say yeah, but Linda, she reaches for the last slice of pizza, takes a bite, throws it back on the plate, and says, 'Now we're done.'"

"Well, we paid for it," said Linda.

As the room filled with laughter, Johnny noticed that Jules, Richie, Becca, and Charlie seemed to be enjoying the story. Even Carl and Gina couldn't help but smile.

"Only, when the waiter starts to take the plate and head toward the kitchen, there's a piece of cheese connecting Linda's mouth to the slice on the plate," said Ed.

"And as he walks away, the cheese gets stretched and stretched," added Linda.

"It comes right at my neck. Like when the dude in *The Godfather* kills Carlos in the car with a piece of wire around his neck."

Everyone laughed as Ed demonstrated ducking from stringy cheese.

As they settled down, Carl said, "It was Clemenza. Clemenza killed Carlo. No 'S.'"

Johnny looked at Carl like, *What? Who cares?*

There was an awkward beat, and then Richie turned to Becca, "I heard what happened at your school, kid. I'm so sorry."

"Thanks, Uncle Richie," said Becca.

The uncle title was more a term of endearment and respect for Johnny's good friend. The two men had met decades earlier when they were just six, so as far as they were both concerned, they were each other's family.

Over the years, Richie and Johnny had been through the good and the bad together. When Johnny's dad hit the whisky too hard, Johnny would hide out at Richie's house until things settled at home. At each other's weddings, the other acted as Best Man. When Jules gave birth to Gina and Johnny couldn't make it back from overseas in time, it was Richie who held her hand in the OR. When Richie's older brother got a life sentence for killing a man during a botched bowling alley robbery, it was Johnny who drove Richie to court every day. When both Becca and Charlie were born, Richie was the one who brought cigars to the hospital. When Richie's wife, Kay, left him, Johnny got him drunk. It was Richie who gave the eulogy for Johnny's sister, who died in a car accident forty years before, and Johnny had eulogized both of Richie's parents when they passed away.

"I'm just sorry that you had to see such ugliness. You'd think in 2016, you could be spared that kind of ignorance," said Richie.

"Just disgusting," said Linda.

Johnny was annoyed but not totally surprised when he noticed that Ed raised his eyebrows and tilted his head at Linda and Richie's remarks. As if he, what? Disagreed? What a moron.

Becca didn't want to talk about it anymore, so she changed the subject. "To make it even worse, they just eliminated the Debate Club, which totally blows," said Becca.

"Language," said Gina.

Becca made a face at her mom. Johnny laughed.

"I didn't know they got rid of Debate. You must be so disappointed," said Jules.

"I am. We were supposed to go to Boston for a big competition, and now that's been canceled. They said it has something to do with funding, but the football team got new bleachers last week, so I think they're full of—"

Becca paused to smirk at her mom, who was looking at her.

"—leaky, wet diarrhea."

Gina shook her head in disgust, but Johnny found it funny.

"You mean that kind after you eat too much fruit or like a bowl of beans?" asked Johnny.

Charlie and Becca both smiled at their grandfather.

"Wonderful table talk, Dad," said Gina.

At the same time, Jules, who had been drinking since noon, went for some more wine and accidentally knocked the bottle over.

Jesus Christ, Jules.

Johnny watched Richie wipe up the spill with his napkin while Jules tried to act nonchalant.

"Maybe it's a good time for coffee," suggested Johnny.

Jules stood up and said, "Good idea. Who wants?"

"I'll take some," said Ed.

"I'd love some, Mom," said Gina.

Carl turned to Jules. "Can we talk about dessert? I'd bet there are some of those rainbow cookies somewhere."

"I forgot," said Jules, looking at Johnny, "I have to hide them from this one."

When Jules went to grab some dirty plates, Gina gestured to her kids, who immediately sprang up to help her clear the table.

"Sit, sit," said Jules.

"They can sit after they help. Besides, if we help you carry all this into the kitchen, we can help find those cookies that much quicker," said Carl.

Jules smiled, picked up her half-full glass of wine, and downed it. And with that, she, Charlie, Becca, and Carl headed to the kitchen.

As soon as Jules was gone, Gina looked at Johnny and said, "What's up with Mom lately?"

"Whattya mean?" replied Johnny, even though he knew what she meant.

"She's been drinking a lot."

You think?

"No. She's fine."

"Yes."

Johnny turned to Richie.

"I mean . . ." is all Richie said. But Johnny knew his face well enough to read that he, too, thought that maybe Jules was hitting it a bit hard.

Johnny covered for her. "Look, she's had a lot on her mind lately . . . getting the house ready for everyone . . . the gifts and all this cooking. We're not as young as we used to be. Plus, I think that with the cold weather, she's just a little overwhelmed and has the blues. Holiday blues. Once we hit the new year, she'll snap out of it. Believe me."

But he knew it was more than that. He knew Jules was depressed, he knew why, and, despite what he said, he wasn't sure she was ever going to "snap out of it."

Luckily for Johnny, Richie distracted Gina with a "How's work?"

Unluckily for Johnny, when Gina turned to Richie, Ed leaned in and said, "You know you still owe me five hundred for a new bumper."

"Five hundred? Take a walk," said Johnny.

"Maybe I should talk to your wife. She seemed surprised in church last week when I mentioned it."

"Go ahead. She'd have done the same thing if she had the chance. Hell, she might have put a bullet in you if she had seen what it said."

Ed contemplated this and shrugged in agreement. "I believe that may be true. But what about Bill Rogers? I'm sure he'd love to know that you're firing live rounds into people's trucks."

Johnny rolled his eyes. He knew Ed could be a prick, but he doubted his friend would call the cops on him.

On the other hand . . .

"You take it to Jake's, and I'll pay whatever he charges to fix it. But I'm telling you now, it ain't going to be near five hundred," said Johnny.

"We'll see," said Ed.

A few seconds later, Jules came back with the dessert.

Johnny used the moment to get away from Ed. He stood up and started to clear the rest of the plates. He was about to grab Richie's when he noticed it was still full of food.

"Richie, you still working on this?"

"Nah. I'm good."

"You hardly touched your meal," said Jules.

"Nothing personal. Upset stomach is all."

"No wonder you're wasting away. How about some dessert?"

"Wouldn't miss it."

There were smiles all around as coffee was drunk and cookies were eaten. Eventually, the conversations petered out, and not long after, Ed and Linda said their goodbyes.

After the Grigsbys left, everyone else chipped in to clean up. Once the table was fully cleared and the dishwasher loaded, they headed to the basement for a nightcap and a "friendly" game of ping-pong.

Becca picked up the paddles first, turned, and looked at Johnny. "You and me?"

"Are you sure you don't want to pace yourself first? Play someone easier, like your mom or dad? Then work your way up to the house champion."

"Oh. Pappi is feeling a little cocky today. Cute. Let's go, and I'll even let you serve first out of respect for you being so, so, so, so old."

Johnny smiled and served.

This is what he had been looking forward to—Christmas at its best. Dinner was what it was, but with Ed and Linda gone, only family was left. Down in the basement, everything felt much better. Jules had switched from booze to coffee, and Gina seemed less worried. As far as Johnny Colletti was concerned, all was good.

"Hey, Mom. You never said, but did you and Dad pick where you're going on the big trip?" asked Gina.

"Oh, yeah. Your dad bought us an Alaskan cruise as a Christmas present," said Jules.

Gina was grinning ear to ear. "I already knew that. And not to brag, but it was my idea!"

It was true; Johnny had no idea what the hell to get his wife. He was happy when Gina suggested the trip.

"Oh. Well, it's lovely," said Jules.

Johnny served again, but Becca returned it right past him. While he picked up the ball, Becca turned to her mom. "Didn't Grandma want to go on a Safari?"

Jules looked up from her coffee, "Becca."

"Grandma had her heart set on that trip," said Becca just as the ball got past her, adding, "Shit."

"Language," said Carl.

"Play more and talk less. A classic 'ignorance of youth' mistake," quipped Johnny.

Unable to let the Christmas present thing go, Gina said, "A safari would be ridiculous!"

"I did it back in '98. Stunning," said Richie.

Becca and Johnny found themselves in a fierce volley. They were both good and equally competitive.

"In '98, you were younger. No offense, but my mom and dad on a trip like that now? With so much walking and hiking? No way," said Gina.

"Grandma has been talking about that safari for years," said Charlie.

Becca caught the ball mid-air, and Johnny looked legitimately mad. He could not care less about the vacation conversation; he was into the game.

"What was that? It wasn't going out."

Becca ignored him.

"And instead, Pappi and Gail got her an Alaskan cruise because that's what he wants to do." She turned to Johnny. "No offense, Pappi."

Johnny was confused by the entire conversation. "Who's Gail?"

He wasn't an idiot. He could sense the tension but had no idea what it was about. He also didn't understand why Gina was so upset with Jules about hitting the wine pretty hard. As someone who had lived with a raging, often violent, drunk parent, he thought Jules getting tipsy from time to time was benign. Everyone needed to move past the drama and enjoy the holiday.

He snatched the ball out of Becca's hand and then served it past her. "I have no idea what we're talking about anymore. But, little girl, that was my point. Seven, serving eight."

Johnny served, and she smacked it hard. It sailed right past him.

"Eight all."

Damn. She's good.

By the night's end, Johnny was out of it. As he crawled into bed, he let out a steady groan of relief. *Thank God.*

Just as he started to drift into a dream about something to do with a City Island vacation he had taken with his mom as a kid, he felt Jules rubbing his shoulder.

"What is it?"

"I want to ask you something."

"Can it wait? I'm shot."

"No. It can't."

Reluctantly, he sat up.

What the hell does she want now?

"Okay."

"Okay. I know this is going to sound crazy . . ."

"Here we go."

"Shush. I think I figured a way out of the hell I've been living in for the past few weeks. Or, to be more accurate, the past few decades."

"Jules."

"Don't with the 'Jules' right now."

"Fine. What is it?"

It was silent for a good two or three minutes.

Is she going to say something?

Just as Johnny started to close his eyes again, he heard his wife say, "I want to kill him."

"What?"

"I am going to kill the President-elect."

For the love of every goddamn thing that is holy.

"Oh, okay. Sounds good. Merry Christmas."

And with that, Johnny turned over to go to sleep.

"I'm being serious."

Johnny thought it best to ignore his wife.

"I AM BEING SERIOUS!" Jules yelled.

Jesus.

"I'm sure you are."

"I am."

"Okay."

"And I need your help."

"No. No, you don't. You can do this all by yourself. I believe in you," said Johnny, employing as much sarcasm as he could muster.

"Screw you."

"Okay, then, good night."

"You being a sniper is the best advantage I have."

I'm not so sure about that one. I missed Ed's windshield by a mile.

Johnny lay there quietly. He decided to wait her out, a war of attrition. After about two minutes, he heard Jules start to say more but then stop herself.

After a few more minutes, Jules fell silent, and Johnny fell asleep.

CHAPTER 6

FOR A WEEK, JULES STEWED. She knew killing someone was insane, but on the other hand, there was no reason for Johnny to be so dismissive. As mad as she was at him, she couldn't figure out how to do it without him. She was in a true catch-22. And so, for that dreamlike week between Christmas and New Year's, Jules did what she did best: suppressed her needs and slowly accepted defeat. Seventy years of being a people pleaser had trained Jules to erase her own needs from her consciousness. As her mother used to say, "A lady never says no and always says sorry."

On New Year's Eve, when the clock struck midnight, Jules was on the couch in the living room. Johnny had gone to bed an hour earlier, but Jules liked to stay up to watch the ball drop. While she waited, she flipped through all the networks as they played their year-in-review segments. She saw lists, countdowns, and generic panels dissecting and discussing everything from sports milestones to feel-good viral pet videos to the tumultuous election that resulted in her affliction being named president-elect. The more Jules flipped through the channels, the more she was forced to relive the past. Finally, the sphere dropped, and confetti floated over all the young people in Times Square.

At 12:01 am, Jules finished the last of her champagne and made two New Year's resolutions: first, no more drinking, and second, come hell or high water, she was going to convince her husband to help her assassinate the President of the United States.

JANUARY 3, 2017

It was about noon when Jules and Johnny got in the Ford to grab lunch. Johnny turned the ignition, and the deep male voice of a famous thriller writer filled the silence, reading from his latest book. To Jules, his voice sounded like the white noise in an industrial factory. After a while, you get used to it, but it's not pleasant.

When she moaned out loud, Johnny paused it.

"You want me to catch you up on what's happened?"

No, I want you to turn it off and never put it on again. I'd rather stick screwdrivers in my ears than listen to this man's vapid mouth-hole.

"I think I can piece it together. I only missed the few minutes you drove to the Wawa yesterday."

"Yeah, right. Nothing much happened anyway."

The two listened to the crime thriller as they drove past dilapidated barns, barren hills, and acres of old woodland where once-gorgeous maples, black walnuts, and birch trees once stood before being decimated by the spotted lanternfly infestation. Jules closed her eyes and listened to the booming voice tell the story of a male detective who was happily married with three kids but had recently been tempted by a new, younger female rookie he had been training. Jules cringed at the tired narrative and let her mind wander to what it would be like to be with another man. At first, she snickered at the idea of a woman like herself having her first affair at the ridiculous age of seventy, but then she started to entertain the fantasy.

Who would it be with? A stranger? A friend? What about a movie star like Robert Redford? But that doesn't even make sense. How would I even meet Robert Redford? Why would he be in Warrensburg? He wouldn't. Dumb.

Her mind drifted to Tim Decker. She hadn't seen Tim in years, but she had such a big crush on him back in high school, pre-Johnny. Tim was clearly infatuated with her, too, but he never acted on it. At the time, she assumed she had misread his intentions. But as she got older, Jules realized that Tim was just a scared boy and didn't know what to do any more than she did. Back when she was full of wonder and curiosity. Back when her parents and Sheila were still alive.

Ah, the hell with it. That was a million years ago. *Goddamnit, am I so pathetic that I can't even let myself fantasize without ruining it?*

Luckily, Jules' circular internal fantasy and self-hatred were muted when her phone rang. She glanced at the screen and saw it was Gina who never called in the middle of a weekday. She shut the audiobook off and put her phone on speaker.

"Hey, honey, is everything okay?"

"No, it's not. I'm in the car with your granddaughter, who just got suspended from school."

"What?! Is she all right?!" asked Johnny.

"She's fine. She staged a walk-out."

"What? What do you mean?" asked Jules.

"I can tell them," said an excited-sounding Becca.

"Hiya, honey," said Johnny.

"So, Mia and I walked into English class this morning. And sitting in the back row was Dan Braunger."

"He's the Proud Boy?" asked Jules.

"Yeah! So, then Mr. Adams, our English teacher, made us write a reflection on ethos, pathos, and logos because we had just annotated an argumentative essay about expanding the school year, but I couldn't sit still knowing that Dan was sitting behind us."

"Of course," said Jules.

"Yeah, I mean, everyone at school knows it was him and his minions who painted the swastika. Mia and I were like, why hasn't he been arrested or at least suspended? Anyway, at one point, because I kept looking back at him, we made eye contact, and he smiled and fully flashed the white pride signal at me. So, I was like, screw this—"

"Becca!" yelled Gina.

"What did I say?!"

Johnny pulled into a spot at Rocco's and said, "Okay. We're about to get some lunch, so can we cut to the chase?"

Can this man not think about food for one goddamn second?

Gina said, "Long story short, your granddaughter messaged everyone in the school and staged a walkout. Half the students, close to five hundred kids, left—"

"And three teachers!" blurted Becca.

"And three teachers walked out of school and stood outside blocking traffic on Manner Road."

Good for her. Jules was proud of her granddaughter. Rather than being scared or indifferent, she was engaged and standing up for herself and her friends. Why couldn't Gina see that and praise her for once? Becca was doing exactly what she should be doing. She was doing the right thing.

"Power to the people!" yelled Becca.

"Damn right!" said Jules.

"Mom!" said Gina.

There was a pause, and then Johnny said, "Well, if there's anything we can do…"

He wants to get her off the phone so he can get his stupid sandwich.

"That's why I called. I have to work tomorrow, and so I need you two to keep your eye on her to make sure that she doesn't get up to no good, especially—"

"I'm the only one not up to no good!" interrupted Becca.

"Mom?" asked Gina.

Jules looked to Johnny to decide.

He nodded.

"Of course."

"Thank you, thank you, thank you. Okay, gotta go. We're home. But I can drop her off at your house by 8:15 tomorrow. And thanks. I love you."

"Love you. And Becca, I'm proud of you," said Jules.

"Mother, please don't encourage her."

After Jules hung up, Johnny said, half under his breath, "Mothers and daughters."

"Yeah."

At least they talk to each other. At least Becca knows that no matter how much her mother annoys her, Gina loves her. She works fifty-plus hours a week and still finds the time to go to all of Becca's debates. She never misses a single parent's night at school. That was not at all the way Jules grew up. *Mom was a mom and a housewife in title only. I swear that woman resented me being born from day one. Today, they'd say she was on the spectrum, and who knows, she could get help or at least understanding. Or maybe they would say she had PTSD from being raised by an abusive father and alcoholic mother. Who knows?*

Thinking about how Becca was raised, or even how she and Johnny had tried to raise Gina, made Jules realize just how insane her parents were.

There were only three of us in that small house for all those years, and we hardly ever spoke to one another. I know it could have been much worse. My dad never hit me like Johnny's dad hit him when he drank. He just wasn't around. I imagine being a policeman was hard for him, but I don't ever remember him setting foot in my school. We never went on a vacation. He was at the dinner table every night, but I don't remember him saying anything. Good or bad. After Mom died, it was worse. He became a ghost of a ghost.

Suddenly, Jules looked up, and, to her surprise, Johnny had already left the truck. She looked out the window and saw him inside the sandwich shop, waiting for her.

Whatever.

Johnny ordered the same thing he always ordered: a large buffalo chicken cheese hoagie and a Diet Coke. Jules settled on a small tuna and a cup of water. The cashier handed them their drinks and asked them to give it five or six minutes for the food. They grabbed their usual booth, and as Johnny sipped his Diet Coke and scrolled through his phone, Jules took a magazine out of her bag and searched for an article to read.

The man can't resist being in charge. If he thinks I will do it without him, he will join in just to show me that he knows more about everything than I do. That's how I'll get him.

Without looking up from her *Better Housekeeping,* Jules said, "I thought you should know, even though you're not going to help me, I am going to kill him."

Johnny either didn't hear her or pretended not to. Either way, Jules was pissed. Was she so wishy-washy that he thought he could will her to shut up?

"You're not going to say anything?" asked Jules.

Then he exhaled, rubbed his eyes, and looked up at Jules.

"Please let this go. Please."

"You know what he did to Sheila back when we were young."

"I get it. Believe me. But what can be done?"

"Look at this nonsense at Becca's school. Our granddaughter is advocating for herself. I want to stand up for myself, too! It's not like he doesn't deserve to die."

"I ain't arguing that," said Johnny.

"So then, let's kill him," said Jules.

"Sure. Why not?"

"I'm serious."

Johnny laughed. "Oh, you are, are you?"

She kept on staring right into his eyes. She was, in fact, dead serious.

Johnny lowered his head. "Wow. I mean, I knew this day would come. It's not like we're getting younger or haven't seen it happen to our friends. I guess I just thought we had a few more good years before one of us lost their entire goddamn mind."

She rolled her eyes at him and took a sip of her water.

"You think . . . you know, back then, that I didn't want to destroy him? Sheila was my friend too. Trust me. I wanted to crack his skull," he added.

She knew he wasn't done yet.

"But Richie talked me out of it, and he was right. What good would it have done? It would have landed me in jail. Then we'd all suffer more."

"Not so sure you being in jail is exactly 'me' suffering." Jules joked.

He smiled.

I got him!

"All things being equal, if I can come up with a solid plan, could you make the shot?" she asked.

"A solid plan?! Really? A solid plan to murder a man?! I mean, just talking about it with me in a public place is nuts."

Johnny looked around to indicate that anyone could hear what they were saying.

He accentuated his point, "You're nuts, is what you are."

"He is a goddamn monster."

Johnny looked at Jules and tried to smile at her, but instead, his lips just kind of quivered.

"It doesn't even matter. You could have the best plan in the world, and we'd never get away with it."

"But let's say, hypothetically, that I figure it out. Could you make the shot?"

Johnny stuck his tongue out and made a fart noise.

Jules waved her hand at Johnny's face as if he were a fly and she wanted him to go away. He rolled his eyes and returned to watching DIY home repair videos on his phone. Eventually, she went back to her article.

Shortly after, the door swung open, and two thirty-something men came in. Both guys had a full-on meathead vibe. To Jules, they looked like the type who spent summer days in different parking lots around town smoking cigarettes, blasting loud music, and being obnoxious. They would sit next to their muscle cars and snicker at people walking by—old, young, short, tall, it didn't matter. If you weren't part of their group, they'd mock you. At best, you felt embarrassed when you walked by them. At worst, you felt scared. The two hooligans approached the counter, looked the waitress up and down, and snickered.

"Hey, sugar. Can I get a Badda Boom and an iced tea? Extra sweet," said Meathead Number One.

"You got it." She looked at the other guy. "And for you?"

"Can I get a chicken parm, and can I grab your number?" said Meathead Number Two.

The cashier looked confused. "What?"

"I was asking if I could get your number."

"Oh, that's nice. But I'm in a relationship."

Long pause.

"I'm sorry, what was your order again?"

"I'd like a chicken parmesan and . . ."

He took another long pause and then added, "And instead of your number, I could just come behind the counter and grab you."

The cashier looked stunned as Meathead Number One slapped Number Two on the back. The two men both started laughing as though they had just said the funniest thing in the world.

Jules felt rage inside her. She looked at Johnny. *Do something!* Johnny looked up but did nothing. Would he intervene if the two clowns pushed it further?

"Qué pasó? No comprende?" said Meathead Number Two.

The cashier looked triggered. She was frozen.

Okay, that's enough.

"Honey, are you okay?" said Jules.

"She's fine, old lady. Just a joke, you know. "

Now Johnny got up and started walking toward the men. *About time.*

"Is there a problem?" Johnny said.

"Why? What are you gonna do about it?"

Just as Johnny got ready to engage, a twenty-something big guy who had been in the back making the sandwiches bolted up front and stood between Johnny and the Meatheads.

"You two need to leave now," said Big Guy.

Everyone froze for a few seconds.

"Right now," repeated Big Guy.

"Okay, hombre. Lighten up," said Meathead Number Two.

They both started to leave. They were still laughing, but definitely more nervous. When they were out the door, the cashier went to the back, and Johnny sat at the table. Jules looked up at him, and they just stared at each other for a moment.

Johnny looked deflated. As Jules tried to make eye contact, he looked out the window.

He's avoiding me.

Rather than call him out, she followed his gaze and saw the two idiots in the parking lot laughing and high-fiving each other. The arrogant, toxic stupidity of the two men reminded her of that night when Sheila lay frozen in her bed and that asshole winked at Jules before leaving the room.

She knew that Johnny felt angry and ashamed about not doing anything back then. But what could he have done? *What could any of us have done?*

When Johnny turned around and saw the cashier crying in the back of the restaurant, his face changed. He sat up straight, and Jules couldn't believe the words that came out of his mouth, "Hypothetically, if you could figure out how to do it and how to get away with it—"

Johnny paused and looked out the window again. "I could one hundred percent make the shot."

As they ate, Jules vomited her thoughts on how to commit the perfect murder. She talked about escape routes, how to be unseen, cameras, DNA, and everything she had seen in her crime shows over the years.

After a while, she could tell she was losing Johnny, so she stopped talking.

They finished their lunch in silence.

CHAPTER 7

ON WEDNESDAY MORNING, JOHNNY WOKE up feeling he had dreamt the entire thing. There was no way he would promise his wife that he would help her kill the president—no way.

Did I say that? What the hell is wrong with me?

He was disappointed that he had let his emotions get the better of him. He should know better than to humor his wife's kooky revenge fantasy. If he was being completely honest with himself, he wasn't even sure he could make the shot, given his aim at Ed's windshield. Sure, he hadn't used his Winchester, and he was a little snockered, but still, that was an easy shot. And he missed.

He shook it off. Jules hadn't brought it up in the two days since, so the whole ordeal was probably over. Downstairs, he and Jules ate their breakfasts in silence, and all seemed back to normal.

"We have to meet the girls at Wegmans."

"I thought she was going to drop Becca off here?"

"Gina has some work to do, and it's just easier for her. I need to do some shopping anyway."

"Fine."

When they pulled up to the supermarket, Johnny contemplated telling Jules he would stay in the car and listen to his book but then decided to go in to make sure that some Apple Danish found its way into the cart.

On their way across the parking lot, Jules said, "Okay, before we see the girls, I wanted to say that last night I thought it all out and think I have a pretty good plan to kill the bastard."

And just like that, Johnny's morning turned to crap.

"Yeah. Look, I was—"

Johnny was interrupted by Gina's hand on his shoulder.

"Hey, Dad."

"Sweetie."

"Thank you again for doing this."

Jules, whom Becca embraced, said, "An opportunity to spend more time with our granddaughter. Our pleasure!"

Gina explained the turmoil at Franklin & Franklin—something about a new district manager being upset with how Gina's supervisor was running things. Blah, Blah, Blah. Johnny couldn't follow a single word of what she was saying. He knew she was a Senior Technical Writer for the pharmaceutical company. He knew she made more money in a year than he made in five at Goodyear. But that's where his understanding and interest waned. He was very proud of his daughter's work ethic and ambition. She thrived at her job and seemed actualized in a way that pleased Johnny. But nothing was more boring than corporate speak and inner office politics.

"Dad?"

Oh crap, she caught him zoning out.

"I'm listening," he lied.

Gina smiled, kissed her parents, and then zipped away.

Inside the store, the threesome walked around as Jules rattled off items from the shopping list app on her phone.

"Sweetie, why don't you go pick out a cereal you like, and we'll meet you in the bakery section."

Becca smiled and darted away, no doubt eager to pick out a crappy sugar cereal that her mother wouldn't allow in her house.

Jules turned to Johnny. "So, what's the furthest distance we can be for you to make a good shot?"

At first, Johnny had no idea what she was talking about.

"What?"

"I'm asking, how long is your range? Like, how many yards could you shoot him from?"

"Oh, good God. Are you really asking this right now, here?"

"Yes, I really am. I know you said you missed what you were aiming for on Ed's car. That can't happen with our—" she looked around, leaned in, and whispered the rest, "—our assassination. We'll only get one chance to get it right."

Johnny didn't want to talk about this at all. And he certainly didn't want to have a conversation about premeditated murder in a public place.

"Come on. Can we please—"

"Somebody has to put this man down. Why shouldn't it be me?!"

"There are a million answers to that question."

"Give me one."

She must be crazy.

"Seriously. Give me one," Jules repeated.

Johnny went through all the reasons in his mind but figured appealing to Jules' strait-laced personality was his best option.

"Well, I hate to say the obvious, but you are the only person I know who comes to complete stops at stop signs. You've never even shoplifted a piece of candy, and now you want to commit the most complicated of all crimes."

"Oh, shush."

"No. I'm not saying that as a negative thing. Your honesty is one of the things that I admire about you. It's just that greater, more devious minds than yours have tried and failed to do what you're proposing."

"I'm not proposing. I am doing."

"But you are proposing that I help you."

"I need your help, and besides, you gave me your word."

"Would you listen to what you're saying? You're talking about this like I promised to take out the trash. Killing someone is different than a chore."

Johnny was dumbstruck when Jules seemingly ignored him. She was distracted by a display of low-fat mayonnaise on sale.

"Now that is a good price," she said.

This woman is unbelievable—the attention span of a squirrel.

After Jules placed two jars in her cart, she turned back to Johnny. "And, speaking of chores, you do need to take out the trash."

Johnny smiled.

On their way to meet Becca at the bakery, Johnny stopped at the butcher's and ordered two steaks. He knew Jules wanted him to cut back on red meat, but he didn't care. When the butcher handed him the wrapped tomahawks, he could feel Jules' judgment.

I don't give a shit!

They met Becca at the bakery where Jules had the baker slice a fresh loaf of whole-grain bread, and Johnny grabbed some Danish.

At the register, Becca scrolled on her phone, and Johnny thumbed through a travel magazine. He wasn't interested in reading the thing. He just wanted to avoid talking to Jules. But hiding in the pages of a Jackson Hole getaway didn't work.

Jules leaned in close and whispered, "If I can get us in a building around the Madison Hotel, can you take him out?"

"Take him out? Who talks that way?"

"I do. So, can you?"

"Oh, for the love of God, what does it matter?" said Johnny.

"It matters to me."

Stalemate.

"Can I please just enjoy this magazine? I'm loving this article on—"

"Words, words, words."

Johnny threw the magazine back on the rack and started unloading the groceries onto the conveyor belt. As he did, he noticed the steaks weren't in the cart. He looked through everything twice, but they were nowhere to be found. He turned to Jules.

"Where are the tomahawks I picked out?"

"Too expensive. I'm not paying seventy-two dollars for steaks."

"What is my life?"

"Your life is pretty good if you ask me."

Johnny couldn't argue with that.

Then Jules said, "You said it yourself. After what he did to Sheila, you wanted to murder him yourself."

"Yeah. As in, I wanted to beat the life out of him, not actually murder him. It's goddamn hyperbole!"

"Well, I don't speak hyperbole. I say what I mean and mean what I say."

"Good for you, Popeye."

"That's not what Popeye said."

"Yes, it is."

"No, he said, 'I am what I am, and that's all that I am.'"

"Right."

"Idiot."

The thought crept into Johnny's head that his wife might be serious. But he quickly pushed it away. *No way*. It was just a fun, albeit dumb, conversation. He figured that Jules was upset about the fact that her last grandchild was going off to school in a few months. Their friends referred to it as "empty nest part deux."

That must be it. Fear is fueling idiocy, thought Johnny. *In time, she'll get over it.*

He whispered, "This is fun talking and all, but even if we pulled it off, we'd never get away with it. There's got to be security cameras all around there. It would take even a dumb cop about fifteen minutes to figure out that the ex-military sniper seen on CC footage entering the hotel was the guy who pulled the trigger. Not to mention that everyone in this supermarket has probably heard us talking about it."

Jules looked up, annoyed. "Stop mumbling. I can't hear a goddamn word you're saying."

Johnny pursed his lips.

Without looking up from her phone, Becca said, "Pappi said that if he's going to shoot him outside of the Madison Hotel, having access to somewhere nearby doesn't matter because you'd both probably still get caught and go to jail."

Jules and Johnny looked at each other. *Busted.*

"What do you expect? You two are practically yelling," said Becca.

"No. You heard us wrong," replied Jules.

"Yeah. We definitely were not talking about assassinating the President of the United States in front of our innocent granddaughter in line at Wegmans. That would be beyond inexcusable. It would be downright idiotic," said Johnny.

"Ignore him. It's only a silly game we play. Imagining what it would be like to do something crazy, like rob a bank. Or assassinate someone. That's all."

"Sure it is. And FYI, my friend Mia's brother, Jordan, works at the Marriott across the street from the Madison Hotel. I bet he could set you up good," said Becca.

Jules looked at Johnny first. "Leave our getaway to me."

"Oh boy," said Johnny.

Jules looked at Becca. "And you cannot tell your mom," said Jules.

"What? That I'm helping you shoot a man?! Yeah, I'm pretty sure I know not to tell my mom."

Johnny looked at the cashier, "What about you? Do you want to help us plan the perfect murder?"

The cashier smiled but looked confused.

Jules hit Johnny on the back of his shoulder.

At the truck, as Johnny unloaded the bags from the cart into the back, Jules reached into her coat and pulled the two steaks out of her inside pocket.

"What the holy hell, Jules?" said Johnny.

Jules also pulled out a head of romaine lettuce, double-A batteries, and a bottle of cranberry juice. She flipped the ill-begotten goods into one of the bags.

"Still think I'm too goodie-goodie to commit a crime?"

Johnny was surprised and slightly impressed.

Becca high-fived her grandma.

"I can do my part. All you have to do is make the shot."

CHAPTER 8

A FEW DAYS LATER, JULES sat on a bed in a room in the downtown Philadelphia Marriott, feeling pretty good about herself. It only took her promising Johnny that she would bake his favorite apple cake to get him to come—that and her playing on his dread of becoming obsolete.

Simple.

Jules knew all too well about the invisibility of age and how most people dismiss the elderly as quaint but not essential. She knew Johnny had felt useless since retiring, and, though she empathized with him, she had always felt that way about herself. It was nothing new. For Jules, the crappy part of aging was her inability to stay as fit as she used to. When she was younger, she'd go up and down the stairs in their house fifteen to twenty times a day. Now, even if she wanted to go up to clean or do some crafting, she often stayed on the couch because it was easier.

She looked at Johnny staring out the window, down three stories at the Madison Hotel's back entrance. She knew exactly what he was thinking; he was questioning his accuracy. He was feeling feeble after missing the mark when he fired at Ed's truck.

As much as Jules felt bad for him, she was not above using his self-doubt as a tactical advantage. If the man thought he had something to prove, he would prove it. The Johnny she knew was a machine and able to do anything he put his mind to. Be it driving twenty hours without a bathroom break to help Gina's family in '07 when they got stuck in Orlando with a broken down car and two sick kids, or doing the Heimlich on a lady with a piece of Mongolian beef stuck in her throat at P.F. Chang's four years ago. Johnny always got the job done. Jules believed in her husband, even if he no longer believed in himself.

"It's pretty nice in here," said Jules.

Johnny ignored her.

"The lobby alone. Did you see those free bikes in the lobby? How neat is that?"

"I don't know. Why do you need a bike if you're in a hotel?" said Johnny.

"For fun. Exercise."

"Seems wasteful."

"You seem wasteful."

Jules looked around the room, appreciating how vibrant everything felt. The mid-century wooden bed frame, matching nightstands, and two large, dark green retro lamps all made sense to her. Even the artwork on the walls was not traditional, generic prints of boring sunsets and mountain ranges. Instead, there was a stunning round mirror above the bed with silver starbursts shooting in every direction. Black and white photos of men and women walking through snow in a city hung above the lovely cherry redwood desk.

"Do you think they change the photos depending on the season?" asked Jules.

"What do you mean?"

"Like, in the summer, do you think they have pictures of people swimming or something instead of people walking in the snow?"

"That's insane. If they do, that means they pay some guy to change the pictures. That guy's job is why places like these are so expensive. Give me the same damn pictures all year long and charge me a reasonable rate. That's what I say."

What a crank.

"It feels so young here—the '60s furniture notwithstanding—with all the young people in the lobby and restaurant."

Johnny looked over at her on the bed. "You say that as if it's a good thing."

"Oh, hush. Change is good."

"Says you."

Jules curled her lip and made a face at Johnny, who lowered his head and took a deep breath.

"Jules, this is fun and all. Seriously, the excitement of planning and pretending like we're going through with it is a gas. I'm enjoying myself. But—"

"Let me stop you there. I'm not pretending."

He cringed and waved her off.

"You'll see; I've got a foolproof plan. Just trust me, would ya?"

"Would you listen to yourself? 'A foolproof plan.'"

Jules pursed her lips together without looking up from her phone and made a fart noise.

"Oh, real nice."

"You already said you would help me. So, can we please stop having this argument?"

"I never said I *would* do it. I said I *could* do it hypothetically. As in, hypothetically, I could do that crazy thing if I were, hypothetically, as crazy as you."

Why don't you hypothetically walk off a non-hypothetical bridge?

Jules looked at her phone and saw a message from Becca.

"They're on their way back here now."

"They," said Johnny, throwing his arms up.

"What?" said Jules.

"'They' is reason 560 why this is FUBAR."

"What is?" said Jules.

"This was already crazy sideways when it was just you and me. But let's put that all on hold for now. With Becca and her little friend's brother knowing about it, we might as well drive ourselves to the cops and call it a day."

"Give it a rest."

But Jules knew he wasn't wrong. She never meant to involve her granddaughter, let alone her friends. She knew she had to devise a plan to get rid of them. But all that could be done later. For now, she just needed to get a feel for the hotel and make sure she could execute the idea, or at least execute it enough to get Johnny on board. His naysaying was starting to wear her down.

Soon, the hotel door opened, and Becca, Mia, and Mia's brother Jordan walked in. While Johnny and Jules had met Mia dozens of times, they had only met nineteen-year-old Jordan once or twice, and they were not fans.

He was wearing sunglasses and brightly colored, tight-fitting clothes. Jules thought he looked like a goof but knew better than to engage in that conversation with Johnny.

All three of the teens were eating candy bars. "Sorry, my blood sugar was off the charts," said Jordan.

"You two shoulda come. Jordan used his keys in the machine, and we got free candy," said Mia.

Jordan flashed the hang-loose hand gesture. Becca took a bite of her Twix.

"So, we gonna kill this d-bag or what?" said Mia.

"You know what? That's enough for me," said Johnny.

He started toward the door, but Jules stopped him.

"Okay. So, if everything goes as planned, there may come a time when the authorities need to talk to you three. I assume there are cameras around here, and when they go through the footage, they'll see you in this room with us."

"True, true. Big brother is everywhere," said Jordan.

"We need a reason that makes sense for you to say why you would be here right now with us," said Jules.

"You mean other than planning the crime of the century," said Johnny.

"Shush," said Jules.

"Can't we say that you were looking to have a romantic staycation, and since I knew someone who worked here, we all came to check out the rooms?" suggested Becca.

"Oh yeah! Old people are always scared to spend money. We say you had to see it first," said Mia.

"Minus the old people crack, that works. We can say we looked at the room and changed our minds," said Jules.

"Not to be the voice of reason at your crazy party, but let's suspend logic, reality, and rational thought for a second. Okay, so the kids have a reason for being here with us. But . . . but they will still know that *we* were here: a former military-trained sniper and someone who has a history with the victim. It will take them less than a minute to determine that we were involved. How do you propose we will get away with this, or am I missing something?"

Maybe that was why Johnny came. He wanted to knock down her ideas. Mr. Unflappable figures that his crazy wife will give up if he pulls her plan apart enough. *Well, he's wrong.*

"I'm working on that."

"Oh. That makes me feel better," said Johnny.

Jules flipped off her husband and then turned to Jordan. "So, as we were saying, we need this room on the 27th, and we thought that we should check in the week before under an alias, so it's all set. Let's say, Monday the 16th. That way, we can come back and store something here."

"Store what?" asked Mia.

"A gun," said Jules.

Johnny corrected her, "A rifle."

Mia mimed shooting a rifle. Johnny shook his head.

"Why not just bring it in a suitcase?" asked Jordan.

Jules looked at Johnny. "Can we do that?"

"No. The padded case protects the accuracy of the telescopic sight, and the stock is meticulously designed and calibrated for firing from a prone position. The instability of being in a suitcase would likely damage the shot's accuracy."

Jules suspected that might be pure bullshit. She knew the rifle case was lined with foam to protect the rifle, but she could easily fit the pieces in a suitcase if she wrapped the components in protective cloth or even bubble wrap. Johnny probably lied because he planned to wear her down, as he had a million times before. *Asshole.*

"Can you just carry the gun case in like it was luggage then?" asked Becca.

"You want to take this one?" said Johnny to Jules.

Jules was confused.

"Go ahead, Ms. Lee Harvey Oswald, tell the kids why we can't carry a gun case through the hotel lobby."

"Oh, shush."

Jules explained that walking through the lobby holding a giant, army-green metal case might draw too much attention. Too many people in their neck of the woods could identify a rifle case and might start asking questions. When Jules added that, in her estimation, walking the rifle through the front doors was too big of a risk, Johnny laughed out loud.

"I wish you could hear yourself."

Jules shushed him and then explained that Jordan had told her that the employees' entrance on the side of the building was the quietest and the only entry without cameras. The best part was that it was right next to the laundry room. Jules figured that she and Johnny could drive the rifle over one night and put the case in an oversized, industrial laundry bin. Then Jordan could wheel it up to their room where Jules could stash it until the day of the convention.

When she finished, Johnny stood up and sarcastically slow clapped.

Jules waved at him to shut up and continued, "The problem is, it's big and has to be hidden somewhere the cleaning staff won't find it."

"Why not just hang a 'Do-Not-Disturb' sign on the door?" asked Mia.

"For a week? We want to avoid any suspicion whatsoever," answered Jules.

"Paranoid much," said Mia.

Jordan looked up and said, "You know, in my parents' basement, we hid all sorts of contraband in the ceiling tiles."

Johnny and Jules looked up. There were no ceiling tiles in the hotel room. It was all drywall.

Johnny turned to Jordan, "Just a thought, but did your mom smoke while she was pregnant with you?"

"Um, how would I know? I was not even born yet!" said Jordan.

Johnny looked at Jules. "Are we actually planning a crime with Generation F'd?"

"Um, not F. We're Gen Z," said Jordan.

Johnny shook his head once more as he snatched a bottle of Jack from the honor bar and downed it.

"That costs, like, eight bucks," said Mia.

Johnny reached into his wallet and tossed fifty dollars on the bed. "That oughtta cover the next six."

"Damn," said Jordan.

Everyone acting like fools started to distract Jules from her plan. It was time to get everyone focused. She went to the window, looked at the hotel across the street, and then turned to look at her husband.

Question his virility. Play on his self-doubt. His arrogance is his weakness.

"Could you hit him from here?"

"With my eyes closed," said Johnny.

"Okay then."

She sat on the bed again and studied the room. The giant green lamps seemed perfect. She leaped up, took a tape measure from her fanny pack, and measured the oversized lamp on the nightstand. That's it. She could cut the back out, hide the rifle in it, and glue it back up. Easy-peasy.

"Do you think this would work?" Jules asked Johnny.

"For what?" questioned Johnny.

"To hide your rifle in," said Jules.

Johnny raised his arms to indicate a resounding, "whatever."

Jules took it as a "yes."

"Jordan, I'm going to need to borrow this lamp," said Jules.

"Are you trying to get me fired?" said Jordan.

"It would be a nice benefit," said Johnny.

Jules smacked Johnny's back. "Now, Jordan, you said you had a laundry chute up here. Can you take us to it, please?"

Johnny and Jules followed Jordan, Becca, and Mia down the hallway.

Jules was animated. "It will be nice. The night before, we can have a fancy dinner and watch some TV."

"Yeah, yeah. Steak and a twice-baked potato, and then for dessert, murder."

Just as Johnny spoke, a good-looking, twenty-something couple walked by.

Mia whispered to Johnny, "Maybe you two should talk about this privately."

"Yeah. Like, I get that you may be hard of hearing, so you have to talk loud. My Nana does the same thing, but like, you are talking about criminal activity in a public place at a particularly high decibel," said Jordan.

The kids had a point.

Johnny said, "The only advantage of getting old is that no one notices you. Gray hair and wrinkles make us invisible to the rest of the world. I could scream, 'I AM GOING TO KILL THE PRESIDENT OF THESE UNITED STATES OF AMERICA,' and no one would give a rat's asshole."

Is he insane?!

Two women walked by, and Jules stiffened, expecting them to say something. She wasn't the only one put off by her husband's remarks. It was clear from the kids' contorted faces that they, too, were uncomfortable with Johnny's outburst.

When the strangers had passed by, seemingly oblivious to Johnny, Jules perked up.

"See, it's old people's superpower. No one cares enough about us to notice us," said a slightly cocky Johnny.

Jules smacked him on the back and said, "Anyway, after you shoot him, we run down this hallway and jump in the laundry chute."

"Jump? In the laundry chute?!" said Johnny.

"Yeah. I figured it all out. We can't go through the lobby because there are cameras in there and out front, right? So, we slide down the laundry chute and escape out the employee entrance. Right, Jordan?"

"Correct-a-mundo."

Johnny added his two cents, "I mean, that's great. Except, they'll have us on camera when we check into the hotel. So even if they don't see us leave, they will have footage of us coming in. Again, it's not hard to put together my military record with our presence at the hotel—bing, bang, boom. Allenwood Penitentiary, here we come."

"That's why we show up in disguises."

"Oh, of course," said Johnny, again reeking of sarcasm.

"Jordan will check us in under a different name, and we will come wearing costumes. Obviously, after shooting him, we can't go out through the lobby, so we will go through the laundry chute."

"Oh. Obviously. Costumes. Laundry chute. My bad. Great idea," said Johnny.

"Shush. In the laundry chute, we could slide to the ground level, where we would have stashed a motorcycle. Preferably a stolen one that we ride to the sewer—"

"Wait. Why a stolen motorcycle? We have a perfectly good one in our garage."

He wasn't wrong. Sheila's old bike was in their garage. Jules hadn't looked at it in years because it symbolized too many painful memories, but she knew Johnny kept it tuned up.

"Because if we use Sheila's old Triumph, they'll trace it. Even if we change the plates, there are only so many '65 Triumphs still around."

"I didn't realize I was married to such a crime boss. Tony fucking Soprano over here," said Johnny.

"Like, how, may I ask, are you going to steal a motorcycle?" asked Mia.

"Grandma and I have been watching DIY hot-wiring videos on YouTube," said Becca.

"Sweet," said Jordan.

"We should all shoot ourselves right now and eliminate the middleman," quipped Johnny.

As much as Jules was annoyed with Johnny's hostile attitude, she admitted there were plenty of holes in her plan. Since her scheme was in its early stages, she wasn't worried. She had time to work out the kinks.

At the laundry chute, everyone gathered around it. Jordan held it open and used his phone flashlight to look down.

"It's pretty dark in there," said Mia.

Jordan looked Johnny up and down and then said slowly, "And narrow."

"Is the imp calling me fat?" said Johnny.

If the cannoli fits.

"Is this even safe, Grandma? I mean, there's no way of knowing what it's like in there."

Safe? Probably not. Doable? Absolutely.

Jordan stuck his head inside.

"It is three floors down."

"I hate to say it, but Skippy's got a point," said Johnny.

"Um, my name is Jordan."

"Why don't I go down to the ground level and shine a flashlight up? If you can see it, then we know it's straight down," said Becca.

"That's smart."

"I try."

"Or we could just find out."

Before anyone could notice, Jules hoisted herself into the chute.

Jules felt Johnny's hand on her back as he reached out to stop her. "Let's wait a second before—"

Too late. Jules was already in and screaming as she slid down.

The laundry chute turned at a very sharp angle. The walls were metallic and slippery, and the ride down was dark. Jules fell fast and banged hard against the sides as she did. Eventually, the laundry chute spat her onto a concrete floor.

Her hands scraped the ground, and she had some cuts, but worse was the pain she felt in her back and neck. Absurdly, a giant pile of dirty linens that would have softened her fall lay right next to where she had landed. *Que sera, sera.*

Despite all of that, it was kind of fun—reminiscent of the Log Flume at Great Adventure Amusement Park that she had ridden with Gina when she was a kid. As Jules was about to get up, Johnny came sliding out.

"You did it!" Jules was ecstatic that Johnny had taken the leap of faith.

"Only by mistake, I was trying to stop you. What the—"

She smiled and was about to hug him when she noticed he was not looking at her. He was looking over her shoulder, and he looked freaked out. Following his gaze, she saw what he saw. Standing over them was a pissed-off-looking security guard.

Goddamnit.

CHAPTER 9

THE FIRST THING JOHNNY NOTICED about the man was the shiny silver flask clutched in his sausage-sized fingers. The second thing was the gold badge on his polyester shirt that read, "Jimmy Pagliarulo, *Hotel Security*."

Everything about him screamed ex-cop: the furrowed brow, the basset hound eyes, and the way his free hand rested—all too comfortably—on the flashlight holstered to his belt. Probably P.P.D., and from the looks of it, the retired police officer missed having his service revolver. More than anything, Mr. Pagliarulo had the penetrating stare of a cop; he was a man who could size you up in less than a minute.

Well, that's that.

Johnny knew that if he could see that the man before them was a retired policeman, his wife could also see it. After all, Jules had once lived with one.

MAY 23, 1964

Johnny was wearing a rented tux, standing before Jules' parents' house. He had been so surprised that she had said yes when he asked her to the homecoming dance that he hadn't even considered meeting her family. As he waited in front of their overgrown pachysandra for them to come out for pictures, he could feel his nerves were on overdrive. He held a cardboard florist's box that his mother had surprised him with before he left his house. Inside was a corsage to give to Jules.

Jules came out of the house first and embraced Johnny. He sheepishly gave her the small bouquet, and she pecked him on the cheek.

Maybe this won't be so bad after all.

"My mom will be right out, but my dad can't stay for pictures because he's working the six-to-four tonight."

Johnny knew that Jules' mom was a Sunday school teacher and her dad was a police officer, but that was all he knew about them. Even though Jules was very talkative, she didn't say much about her family. Johnny thought that was weird, but on the other hand, he only had one friend—Richie—so it wasn't like he had a lot of other people to compare her to.

Johnny forced a smile when Jules' mom came out. Given Jules' flair for dressing nicely, he was surprised that for homecoming pictures, her mom wore no makeup, her hair was tied back, and she was wearing an overworn house dress.

"Hello, Mrs. Dayitch."

"Evening," was all she said.

Johnny was even more taken aback when Mr. Dayitch walked out. The six-foot-two man was wearing jeans and a dress shirt, but the .38 and badge in his right hand caught Johnny's attention. The stoic man sat on his front steps, strapped the service revolver to his ankle holster, and fastened his badge to his belt before standing up and smoothing his hair with both hands.

"I may work O.T. tonight. No telling when I'll be back."

Johnny wasn't exactly sure who the man was talking to since he was staring at the horizon as he spoke. On his way to his car, Jules' dad stopped and stared at Johnny with a penetrating, judgy look. After about twenty seconds, he cracked a smile and then without so much as saying, "Hello, nice to meet you," to Johnny, or, "Have a good time," to his daughter, or, "I love you to his wife," he got in his seafront green Chevy Corvair and drove off to work.

It's not even five. He couldn't stay an extra twenty seconds for a picture?

Jules looked at Johnny and whispered, "Sorry."

Over the years, Johnny got to know a little more about Jules' dad. He was sometimes there for holiday dinners, but more often than not, he was working. When her dad *was* there, the man hardly spoke. It's not that he was rude. He was polite and smiled from time to time but was always distant.

Johnny always felt bad for the guy. To him, Jules' dad seemed bored. Johnny assumed he was missing the kind of power and thrill that came with wearing a badge. A cop's entire day was about being in charge. They scared some people and made others feel safe, but no matter what, they were above the rules. Police officers existed outside societal norms. They cut to the front of lines in stores, ran red lights, and flashed their badges to get things unavailable to everyone else. Johnny imagined having that much authority at work made everything else a drag. Furthermore, the heightened sense of their day-to-day, looking for the bad in everyone they met, and the awareness that they could face a lethal interaction at any given moment helped Johnny understand why off-duty cops always seemed annoyed or uninterested.

That said, understanding the man didn't make his obliviousness to his daughter any more forgivable. Jules deserved to have a more present dad. She was poised for greatness, and her own father was too in his head to notice. Whatever his reason, Johnny resented the man for the effect he had on Jules.

JANUARY 7, 2017

Pags stood there looking down at him and Jules with that same dead-eyed stare Johnny had seen at the Dayitch dinner table so many times. He did not doubt that Jules saw it, too.

After a few minutes of silence, Becca and Mia rushed into the laundry room.

Mia surveyed the scene and said, "Uh oh."

Seconds later, Jordan sauntered in. "We did—" he stopped mid-sentence, covered his face with his hands, and backed out of the room before the security guard could see him.

What an idiot.

"Would somebody mind telling me what in the hell is going on here?" said the rent-a-cop.

Let's see Jules talk her way out of this one.

Johnny almost felt bad for his wife, who simply shrugged and looked down at her shoes. Almost.

When Becca stepped forward, Johnny smiled. *This ought to be good.*

Becca squinted at the man's name tag as she tried to pronounce it. "Hi, Mr. Pag-la-roo—

"Jesus Christ. Just call me Pags, and please tell me what is happening here."

"Okay, Pags. My name is Becca, and this is all my bad," said Becca.

"What is?"

"This. Them. It's an Instagram thing," lied Becca.

"What the hell does that mean?" asked Pags.

"Sorry. It's a social media app."

"Kid, I may be old, but I'm not a friggin idiot. I know what Instagram is. I meant, why the hell are they in my laundry chute?"

Good question.

"Oh, yeah. So, like, people all over the country are filming grandparents doing adventurous stuff, like cliff jumping and skydiving, and then posting the videos online. And I begged mine to go down the laundry chute."

The kid's a good liar.

"I worry for your generation," said an annoyed Pags.

"Seriously, you have no idea," said Mia.

Pags stared at Becca and then at Mia. He then turned to Jules and Johnny.

"And you two fools, you did this online stupidness?"

Johnny knew Jules was scared, but he couldn't be happier. Getting caught by an over-eager security guard meant the whole thing was over. Even Jules couldn't argue with the fact that any chance they had at anonymity inside the Madison Hotel was shot to crap.

Johnny grinned as Pags shook his head and grabbed the walkie-talkie from his back pocket.

This ends now. Thank Christ.

"Security to the front desk. Come in."

"Front desk here," crackled a voice over the speaker.

"Edward, I was just making my rounds and thought you should be aware that I apprehended two people doing some social media challenge where they slid down the laundry chute."

"What? Are you serious?"

Pags rolled his eyes. He clearly did not like Edward. "No. I thought it would be so funny to call you and lie about this because, you know, you and I have such a whimsical relationship."

"Okay, no reason to be a grump. Are they college kids or younger?" asked Edward.

"Neither. They're old folks," said Pags.

"What?"

"Like my age."

Okay, that was a stretch because the security guard looked at least ten years older than Jules and Johnny. Just then, Johnny turned to Jules and saw her running her hand through her hair. When she pulled it back, it was covered in blood.

Shit.

"Your head is bleeding," said Johnny.

"What?" said a puzzled-looking Jules.

"I'll call you back in five," said Pags into the speaker.

Johnny walked over to Jules and looked at the cut on her head. It wasn't that bad, but it wasn't good either. They needed to go to the hospital. He looked at Jules, grabbed her hand, and pulled her toward the door.

"Where do you two think you're going?" said Pags.

"We need to get to the hospital," said Johnny.

"Fine. I need to see your IDs before you leave."

"Why?"

"So when the manager calls the cops, he can tell them who you are."

"Cops? No one needs to call the cops," said Johnny. As much as he wanted to put the kibosh on his wife's plan, Johnny didn't want to get the cops involved.

"That's up to Edward, not me."

"Can't you just tell him not to?" said Jules.

"No." He reached his hand out for their IDs, but Jules groaned in feigned pain.

"My grandmother needs to see a doctor," said Becca.

Johnny knew that Pags wasn't an idiot and probably knew they were all full of crap, but it also didn't seem like Pags cared all that much.

In the end, Johnny was right about the rent-a-cop's apathy. He let them go.

CHAPTER 10

ON THE WAY TO THE hospital, Jules forgot about Pags, the hotel manager, and the police. Instead, she focused on what would happen when they got to the emergency room. If the staff knew how they were injured, they might question the "elderly couple's" mental faculties and be suspicious about their behavior.

"We should skip the ER," said Jules.

"Your head is bleeding, and you need stitches. We're not skipping anything," answered Johnny.

"But what if we raise red flags and people start to look into our lives?" said Jules.

"Easy on the melodrama."

"You know what happened last year. My friend Mary went in—"

"Here we go," interrupted Johnny.

"She went in after burning her hand on the stove, and next thing you know, they put her in assisted living," pointed out Jules.

"Mary's brain had also turned to mush."

"That's not nice."

"Sure, but it also happens to be true. I ran into her at Willaby's once, and she thought I was Winston Churchill," said Johnny.

"Well, you have gained weight, and you do love the sound of your own voice."

Johnny scowled.

"I'm only saying that when we get to the ER, we shouldn't tell them how we got hurt," said Jules.

"That's probably a good idea," said Becca.

"No, it's not. There's no good reason to lie," said Johnny to Becca before turning to his wife. "You and I, or at least I, know I could pass any cognitive test they gave me. It's totally different than old, crazy Mary Swansen."

"You're mean. A mean, mean man."

"I can live with that."

I can't.

"And, for your information, I'm not worried about getting committed. I'm worried about them looking into us or sending social workers, or whatever, to our house while we're planning our thing," said Jules.

"It's not *our* thing. *Your* thing is killing the President of the United States of America. Just so there's no illusion about how batshit your thing is when it's said out loud."

Jules stuck her tongue out at Johnny. What a negative man.

"Maybe both of us should be committed—you, for talking like this, and me, for humoring you."

"Oh, shush."

Jules then devised a plan to tell the doctors and nurses that she and Johnny had fallen on the ice. They were walking to the car and fell. *When I went down, Johnny came to help me, and then he fell too. It could happen to anyone.*

The hospital was calm. One thing Jules loved about living in a small rural town was how easy everything was compared to the city. She had visited friends in Philadelphia hospitals over the years, and they were so chaotic and filthy. This ER had oversized recliners in the waiting room, and the TV and magazines were in good shape. There was even decent free hot coffee and donuts. But more impressive to Jules than the creature comforts was the short, eighteen-minute wait before seeing an ER nurse in a clean, fully stocked, and curtained-off examination room.

Minutes later, the doctor walked in. She was in her mid-forties, over six feet tall, and all business as she looked down at her clipboard and said, "Hello, my name is Dr.—"

"I know you. Little Hallie Jackson," said Jules.

"Not so little anymore," added Johnny, looking up at the tall doctor.

Even though Jules hadn't seen Hallie in person in over thirty years, she immediately recognized her. Jules knew Dr. Jackson's mother, Barbara, from church and had been forced to look at countless photos on her phone. Barbara would trap Jules in the foyer and shove pictures of Hallie on vacation or working in South America for Doctors Without Borders in front of her face. The proud mother would go on and on about Hallie's life, including her acceptance into George Washington University, exceptional performance in medical school, and choice to work at the small, local hospital despite multiple offers from more prominent institutions. Jules found Barbara annoying, but then again, Jules found most people to be a pain in the ass.

Doctor Jackson smiled.

She told Jules that she remembered her from when she was a kid. They exchanged a few pleasantries, and then the doctor asked Jules some questions. She did a quick exam and began stitching the minor lacerations on Jules' forehead.

This isn't so bad. Be out of here in no time.

Once Dr. Jackson was done with the sutures, she pushed out half of a smile at Jules.

"Luckily, you don't have any signs of a concussion."

"That's good," said Johnny.

"Take some Tylenol for the pain and put some ice on it to stop the swelling. In a few days, the stitches will fall out on their own, and you should be fine."

The doctor removed her gloves and threw them in the trash can as Jules slid off the gurney and stood up. When Dr. Jackson turned back around, she looked at Jules' legs.

"I can't help but notice that your pants are ripped."

She examined Jules again and pointed out more cuts and bruises on her lower back.

"You two are pretty roughed up for a small fall. Are you sure there's not something you're not telling me?"

"It's like we said, I slid, and then when my husband tried to help me up, I accidentally pulled him down on me, which made it worse," said Jules.

"Did you fall forward or backward?" asked the doctor.

"What? I fell backward. On my derriere."

"That explains the abrasions on your lower back and legs, but I'm still confused about how you sustained the scrapes on the front of your knees. Not to mention how your forehead became bruised."

"What? No. Why? What?" said a flustered Jules.

"Can you explain those other injuries?" asked the doctor.

Jules wanted to say something, but only weird, incomprehensible sounds came out when she opened her mouth.

Why does she even care?

Jules knew that Johnny didn't want to lie to the doctor, but she needed help.

"Johnny, you explain it to her."

Johnny looked annoyed by being put on the spot, but what choice did Jules have? *Just lie, you jackass.*

"No, it's like we said. My wife fell on the ice on our way to the car, and when I went to help her, I slipped as well. I hate to admit it, but I'm not as agile as I used to be, and when I landed on her, that's when I think she bumped her head," said Johnny.

"It's true. I saw them fall. They're pretty old, you know? And Grandpa forgets things a lot," added Becca.

At least Becca can think fast.

Becca hammed it up, "It's okay, Grandpa, we're going to get you all the help you need."

Dr. Jackson looked at them a little warily. "Do you mind if I speak to Mrs. Coletti alone?"

Johnny cringed but said yes.

Once Johnny and Becca left the exam room, Dr. Hallie pulled up a stool and smiled at Jules. "If something is going on at home, you can tell me. We can get you to help."

This took Jules aback.

Could Dr. Jackson possibly know what we're up to? If so, how? No way.

"I'm not sure what you mean," said Jules.

"If anyone is hurting you, you can tell me."

"What?! No," said Jules.

Dr. Jackson put her hand on Jules' shoulder and made direct eye contact. "Are you saying that no one at home is abusing you?"

Abusing me? Is she serious?!

Jules started to laugh.

"I know this can be difficult, but we have resources to assist you if you need help."

"Johnny. Hitting me?" Jules' face turned red, and she began to snort.

"I'm sorry if talking about this makes you uncomfortable."

Jules could not stop laughing. She knew Hallie was serious and that Dr. Jackson had the best of intentions, but her heightened nerves and anxiety were starting to bubble out. The more Jules lost it, the more concerned the doctor looked.

Finally, Jules said, "No, of course not. Johnny would never hurt me. I appreciate you doing your job; your caring is very sweet. I can see why your mother likes to brag about you so much, but you're barking up the wrong tree. My husband is a lot of things, but he has never laid a hand on anyone, and he would never hurt me."

"Domestic violence isn't funny," said the doctor.

You don't have to tell me.

―――――

NOVEMBER 5, 1968

In the dorm hallway, a nineteen-year-old Jules listened on the wall-mounted common phone as her mother gave her the awful news. "I'm so sorry, Jules. It was late last night, and I just found out."

Jules wasn't sure she wanted to know, but couldn't stop herself from asking, "How?"

"I don't know. From what Mrs. Newman told me, Sheila came home early for the weekend."

Jules knew better than anyone that after the incident, Sheila had left school to go home for a few days. Jules felt her absence like a missing limb.

"She was taking some pills to help her sleep. She must have accidentally taken too many," said Jules' mother.

Accidentally.

Jules held the phone to her chest, bit her lip, and cried some more.

When she finally put the phone back to her ear, she could hear her mother calling her name. "Jules? Jules . . . ?"

Okay, take a deep breath. Get it together. Keep moving. Keep moving.

"I'm here. Okay, I will be home tomorrow. I'll call Johnny at the barracks, and if he can't drive me, I'll be on the first bus out of downtown. I have to tell all my professors that I'm leaving, but I'll be there."

"Okay, if you take the bus, call us when you arrive, and your father will come to get you."

"Thanks."

"And please stay as long as you need, muffin."

Muffin? That one caught Jules by surprise.

She sounds almost maternal.

"Thank you. I'll be home at least through the service."

The thought of a funeral somehow made it even more real. Jules needed to get off the phone before she fully lost it.

"Okay, tell Daddy I love him. And I love you too."

She hung up the phone, leaned against the wall, and slid to the floor.

A few minutes later, Jules walked into her dorm room, grabbed a tissue, blew her nose, and pushed the desk chair over to her closet. She pulled down a suitcase from the top shelf, which she immediately became aware was too heavy, and it fell to the floor.

Goddamnit.

With a hug-like grab, she snatched all the clothes hanging in the closet, turned, and dropped them on the bed.

Hold it together.

She wiped her eyes, and then Jules heard, "Hey, Doll."

She turned and saw that the man who had raped her best friend was sitting on her bed.

Jules was stunned. *What's he doing here? How did he get in here? What is going to happen?*

Jules thought her eyes were failing. He was knitting the blanket she had started.

The creep held up the needles and yarn, "Hope you don't mind. I saw this while I was waiting and thought I might as well help you get further along."

"What?! What are you doing in here?! How—"

"I'm waiting for Sheila. She gave me a key."

He doesn't know. He doesn't even know. For what felt like an eternity, Jules sat there frozen.

"She's dead."

"What?"

"She went home after what happened . . . after what you did to her."

Jules was too scared to finish her thoughts. Not that she even had the words.

"What? What did I do to her?"

All Jules could manage to say was, "She went home, and last night she OD'd. And now she's dead."

He looked more annoyed than upset.

Soulless.

"Wow. Oh, I am so sorry. That is just awful," he said without looking up from the yarn in his hands.

Jules stared at the aluminum knitting needles, equally fascinated by how adept he was at knitting garter stitches and that he seemed to have nothing else to say about Sheila.

You killed her. You killed her. You killed her.

"I'm sorry. I don't care how you got in, but you need to leave right now."

"Rude."

"What?"

"You're being rude, Jules. I am very fond of you, despite what you think of me. You're a formidable but sweet lady, and I don't mind saying I'm enamored."

What the actual hell? Is that all he's going to say about Sheila? It had zero effect on him, and now what, he's moving on to whatever's next? Enamored. He's enamored. Sheila's dead. DEAD!

"Please . . ." was all Jules could manage to squeeze out.

He walked over to Jules' nightstand, where there was a picture of a young Johnny in his uniform. He picked up the photo.

"Johnny enlisted. Figures. Between you and me, you have to be pretty lame to join the army. It's probably why we're losing in Vietnam."

Johnny is twice the man you are. And he's in the Navy, you idiot.

"I want you out now."

He smirked and put the photo down, but didn't leave. Instead, he walked over to a baseball bat leaning in the corner of the room. He looked back at Jules and picked up the bat.

"You play?"

The bat had been a gift from Johnny. He gave it to Jules the day she moved into the dorms to—in his words—protect herself. But Jules was too scared to say anything about any of that. She said nothing.

"I could've played pro ball if I wanted to."

Then he took a slow, home run swing.

"I was a good fielder. But I was great with the bat. I could really cream a fastball."

Then time stopped, and all the air went out of the room. One minute he was in the corner of the room, and the next, he was standing over her with the skinny end of the bat in his hand and the fat end against her neck. He twisted and turned the bat into Jules' throat like a screwdriver. It hurt—a lot.

Fight.

When she pushed it away, he laughed, put it down, and fell back onto the bed. For a little while, he just sat there knitting in silence.

Jules, who was crying again, summoned all her strength to say, "Please . . . just leave . . . please."

Once again, he smirked. He had no intention to go anywhere.

Jules knew she needed to do something, but she couldn't. Her body was stuck, and she was incapable of moving. It felt surreal.

This is it . . .

Luckily, there was a loud knock on the door, followed by, "Jules! Hey, it's Marsha. I just heard about Sheila. I'm . . . I'm so sorry."

Jules looked at the door and yelled as loudly as she could, "Come in!"

The door burst open. Marsha came in, he walked out, and Jules collapsed.

JANUARY 7, 2017

Dr. Jackson looked at Jules with weary eyes. "Okay. As long as you're okay."

"I am. I promise you. And I know that domestic abuse is no laughing matter."

"It's not, Mrs. Coletti."

Jules stood up.

"If you ask for help, I can help you."

Johnny and Becca walked back in.

"We all good then?" said Johnny.

"Yes," said Dr. Jackson as she turned back to Jules, "Again, the stitches will fall out in a few days, and please call me if you need anything."

Johnny hurriedly helped Jules but winced in pain when he bent down to get her purse off the floor. Of course, the doctor noticed Johnny's pain and again looked bewildered. Johnny must have clocked the doctor's confusion.

"Arthritis," said Johnny, holding his right hand.

The doctor told Johnny that if the pain worsened, he should ask his GP for a prescription. Johnny and Jules thanked Dr. Jackson, told her to say hi to her mom, and hurried out.

CHAPTER 11

ON THE WAY HOME FROM the hospital, Johnny was furious. He was still angry that Jules had jumped into that chute without thinking about the consequences—she could have killed herself. On top of that, he had overheard Dr. Jackson all but accuse him of abusing his wife. And despite the insanity of it all, Jules seemed undeterred. To her, it was all a big game. The fact that anyone could think that about him stuck in his craw. Johnny was a good man. He wasn't capable of even thinking about what the doctor had suggested. He had spent his life trying not to be like his dad, an angry, violent drunk. When he was younger, Jules suggested he see a therapist to talk about how he had grown up, but Johnny didn't need some college-educated head shrinker to tell him that his entire personality was defined by the guilt he felt for never standing between his dad and his mom. For never stopping the animal that destroyed her life. When his old man's heart gave out, Johnny was only seventeen. He never had the chance to confront him. *Whatever.*

After his dad passed, Johnny went out of his way to confront any man he thought was threatening a woman. He, of all people, saw what that could do to a family, how it could hurt, not only physically, but also cripple a person emotionally. Johnny despised those men. And now, after a life of railing against that toxic energy, to be accused of hurting his wife? No way. Johnny was about to say something to Jules in the car when Becca got a call.

"Hey Mia . . . No, they're fine," said Becca.

"Is that Mia? Ask her if that hotel security guy or his manager reported us to anyone," said Jules.

Of course, he did.

"Put it on speaker so we can hear," said Johnny.

"They want to know what happened at the hotel after we left," said Becca.

"After you guys split, nothing happened," said Mia.

"What do you mean nothing happened?" asked Johnny.

"Um. Like. Nothing happened, is what I mean," replied Mia.

"The manager didn't call the police?" asked Jules.

"No, the security guard covered for you guys. He just said it was a mistake and that everything was fine. We good."

"What? Why? Why would he do that?" asked Johnny.

"Because Jordan stepped up," said Mia.

"What the hell does that mean?"

"Right. It turns out that the old security guard is a bit of a boozer. Jordan, and just about everybody else who works at the hotel, knows that Pags slips into the laundry room every couple of hours to have a few shots."

"No way," said Becca.

"Way," said Mia. "So Jordan went up to him and said, 'Hey, if you decide to tell the manager to call the cops about this, then we should also tell him why you were in there in the first place.' And I guess the old man knew he was beaten because he just said something about one hand washing the other and walked away."

"Sweet," said Becca.

"Right?" replied Mia.

"I only understand about fifty percent of what you two say on any given day. So, let me get this straight. That security guard drinks at work, and because of that, he won't report us?" said Jules.

"Bingo," said Mia.

After Becca hung up, Jules smiled.

"I wouldn't be so happy if I were you," said Johnny.

"Why? You heard Mia. No harm, no foul," said Jules.

"No harm, no foul? Are you kidding me? Right out of the gate, when we tested one of your plans, we were almost arrested by a retired cop. Not to mention that our friend's daughter thinks I'm abusing you."

Jules' smile quickly vanished.

Johnny drove the point home further, "I mean, now, imagine for one second that this isn't just a cockamamie fantasy and that we go through with it. Accepting all that, which I don't at all, but dollars to donuts if we were to kill the guy, the security guard will draw a parallel between the two people of a certain age who slid down the laundry chute just a few weeks before a murder took place in the same hotel."

"First of all, you're an asshole. Second of all, even if he connects the dots, he doesn't know who we are," said Jules.

"No, but you just heard Mia. That nitwit Jordan just went and blackmailed him, so now Mr. Pags can connect us to him. And maybe Pags' fear of getting caught drinking at work will stop him from reporting a bunch of hooligans. But I doubt that indiscretion will stop a retired cop from doing the right thing when it comes to apprehending two assassins!"

Jules looked mad but didn't say anything.

"So maybe, just maybe, I'm not an asshole but a voice of reason in a shitstorm of delusions of grandeur."

Johnny could see that Jules was feeling beaten down. Usually, that would make him stop. He didn't enjoy crushing his wife's fantasy, but it felt like the responsible thing to do this time. He needed to put this to bed once and for all.

"Say that Jordan doesn't give us up, which he would in a heartbeat, believe me. But say that kid somehow toes the line. How long do you think it would take them to track us down just based on our age and the security cop's description of us? Or even better, once they check all the CCTV footage from the street cameras around the hotel from earlier today, they'll have our mugs on the news. Or they will use facial recognition software to identify us from our driver's license photos."

"They can do that?"

"They can and they will."

Johnny actually had no idea if they could do that.

He went on, "But then again, they won't even get that far because once the cops put pressure on Skippy, Mia, and even Becca, they will quickly give us up. And, now, we've got our granddaughter and her friends as accessories. So, the kids can join us in prison."

Jules took a long pause, and Johnny assumed that was the end. He was, of course, wrong.

"Oh, shush, it's just a hiccup. I'll figure it out."

"No. You won't figure anything—"

Johnny stopped himself when he noticed Jules was no longer engaging with him. If there's one thing he'd learned in nearly fifty years of marriage, it was how to recognize when an argument was over. He knew Jules well enough to know that her mind was locked, and there was no way he could change it. Not that it mattered because when push came to shove, he knew she wasn't serious. Even if she was, she couldn't devise a plan that they would get away with. He would poke a hole in any attempt she made. Rather than argue, he decided to let it go.

⸻

Back at home, an hour before dinner, there was enough time to read. Johnny's preferred reading location was upstairs in the office, on the faded, squishy, but comfortable couch. On the wall behind the sofa hung prized photos Johnny had collected over the years: a print of Muhammad Ali standing over Sonny Liston, the famous V-J Day in Times Square by Alfred Eisenstaedt, and a nice print of Philadelphia Eagles Hall of Fame linebacker and center, Chuck Bednarik. None meant more to Johnny than a signed Bob Gruen photo of John Lennon with his NYC tank top from the late '70s. Everyone thought Johnny a fool when he bought it at an auction, framed it, wrapped it, and gifted it to himself as a fiftieth birthday present. Johnny, however, was delighted with himself for that one.

He plopped down on the couch with his copy of François Maspero's *Out of the Shadows: A Life of Gerda Taro*. Listening to audiobooks in the car was fun, but a nice hardcover was still preferable. Plenty of Johnny's friends read on Kindles or listened to books on their phones, but that wasn't reading.

Thrillers were good time-killers in the Ford, but at home, it had to be non-fiction—history, biographies, sports stories, and even contemporary memoirs. And the best reads were always about photography.

As a kid, Johnny dreamed of being a photojournalist. It was just a pipe dream, but when he was eleven, his mother scrounged some money and bought him his first camera. Suddenly, Johnny's impossible dream felt realistic.

After joining the Yearbook Committee in high school, he interned at the local newspaper and even crafted a makeshift darkroom in his bedroom closet. As a kid, that darkroom was his sanctuary and the one place Johnny could escape from his father's alcoholic rages. While some kids had sports, Boy Scouts, or clubs, it was isolation and a voyeuristic search for frozen beauty that occupied Johnny's teen years.

He had considered trying to be a photojournalist during Vietnam, but the path to achieving that seemed confusing and involved. The impatience of youth got the better of him, and he enlisted. It quickly became apparent in basic training that he had a gift for making long shots. He had never shot or hunted with his dad or even fired a rifle before signing up; it just came naturally to him. Since there was no Sniper Scout training for the Navy back then, Johnny trained with the Marines. The Navy tried to convince him to join the SEALs, but Johnny resisted. That all seemed too intense, and he didn't think it was for him. Besides, working with the Marines gave him some status. There was always a bit of rivalry between the two branches, and Johnny had a foot on both sides. Ed was kind of right when he said Johnny was the golden boy back then. He didn't seek the attention, but if he was honest, it was nice. Then the combat happened, and all that shit didn't matter anymore.

Initially, Johnny imagined coming back and beginning a photography career. But coming home and facing the responsibilities of being a parent ended Johnny's creative life. Even so, he still loved the form.

Johnny looked up at Lennon's photo, smiled, and then dove into Taro's biography. Gerda Taro was the first female photographer to film during the war, and her life and work reflected the bittersweet memories that haunted Johnny's dreams. Taro was born in Stuttgart, Germany, in 1910, and by the time she was in her early twenties, she was forced to flee to Paris for not only being Jewish but also publicly protesting and speaking out against the National Socialists. She survived the Second World War, and in 1946, she left Paris for Barcelona to film the Spanish Civil War. While in Spain, Taro and her partner, Robert Capa, more or less invented the genre of modern war photography. Her life tragically ended prematurely when a truck she was riding in crashed into an out-of-control tank. She was a hero to many people and celebrated as an anti-fascist and a feminist. But to Johnny, Gerda Taro was simply an amazing photographer. To him, her photos honestly represented the experience of war more than any others.

His eyes were stuck on a pic. of Taro's from her series titled, "Brunete 1937." Specifically, a gripping photo of young soldiers in the middle of a war, experiencing a moment of stillness while smoking a cigarette. The duality of joy and horror stirred up a lot of feelings, an almost comfortable weight.

The emotional rollercoaster abruptly stopped when Jules yelled up to him, "I'm just about done. Can you bring down your rifle?"

Another peaceful moment was shattered by lunacy.

Maybe if he ignored her.

"JOHNNY?"

It's as if she knows I'm hungry and tired and that I would do anything to avoid a fight right now. Unbelievable.

He returned the book to his desk, grabbed the case from the gun closet, and headed downstairs.

When Johnny walked into the kitchen and saw that Jules had cut the back out of the hotel's ceramic lamp with a straight razor, he stopped in his tracks. Something about the way she looked, her concentration and pleasure, caught him by surprise. Jules' face was animated, and her relaxed body emitted confidence. Johnny just sat back and looked at her with tenderness for the first time in years. So much of their marriage had consisted of arguing about big decisions and tearing each other down over minutiae that their relationship had become almost adversarial. Johnny and Jules had been married for nearly fifty years, and their romantic notion of growing old with someone had been reduced to the harsh reality of growing old without a sense of self. But as Johnny sat in the hallway and looked at his seventy-year-old wife enjoying herself, he felt the ghost of what his marriage had once been. He smiled to himself and walked over to her.

"Why not use the tile saw and vise in the garage?"

"It's too cold out there. This works fine."

"If you say so."

What is my life? My wife and I are flirting while she prepares a lamp to hide a weapon to kill a man. How long do I keep this up? At what point does she come to her senses?

CHAPTER 12

JANUARY 9, 2017

JULES SNUCK OUT OF BED the following Monday without waking Johnny and drove over to Richie's. It was early enough that no one else was out and about, and Jules took advantage of the light traffic and drove extra fast. Johnny had always been a safe and slow driver; Jules, not so much. As the truck kicked up dust, Jules was flooded with memories of her and Sheila flying around their college, wreaking havoc. Back then, everyone had called them crazy because they often raced the green-and-cream trollies around Germantown and did donuts in the library parking lot. And when Sheila would come to stay at Jules' family's house for a weekend from time to time, it was even worse. In Warrensburg, Pennsylvania, in the '60s, two ladies on a motorcycle were considered scandalous.

One Sunday, Jules was supposed to get back to school so she could study for an economics class that was kicking her ass when Sheila asked if she could take a "quick detour."

OCTOBER 1967

"Just for a few minutes. I have a big test tomorrow," said Jules.

"Okay, Einstein," said Sheila.

She didn't understand why academia was a joke to Sheila. It wasn't like she didn't do well at school. Sheila's grades were just as good, if not better, than Jules'. The difference between the two roommates was that Jules succeeded by working her ass off, whereas for Sheila, it came naturally. From Jules' perspective, everything seemed to come naturally to Sheila. She was a fantastic tennis player, she spoke fluent English, Spanish, and French, she could fix any machine, and she cooked French cuisine better than any restaurant Jules had ever eaten at. Most of Sheila's talents stemmed from being curious and becoming obsessed with things in a way that blew Jules' mind. They once took a bus to New York and went to the Café Wha? to see the folk singer Karen Dalton. Within a month, Sheila—who had never picked up a guitar before—could play perfectly half a dozen classics, like "Down on the Street" and "Little Bit of Rain." However, Sheila also had many of these abilities because she had unlimited opportunities. Jules had never met someone who grew up as affluent as her roommate. Sheila's dad was an architect who had designed many office buildings in Philadelphia. Even more impressive to Jules was Sheila's mother, who ran multiple charities and gave so much to so many in need. Everything about the Newmans was foreign and magical to Jules. Sheila's parents worked long hours and had big lives, but they were also there for every parent weekend and tennis match. By contrast, Jules' parents never attended a single parent's weekend.

Jules mostly loved the Newmans because they smothered her with hugs and compliments whenever she saw them. Jules always felt like she belonged when they were around.

"I'm serious. I'll go for a ride, but I have to be back at school by three. I have to study," said Jules.

"Okay, deal," said Sheila.

An hour later, they were careening around Walton Lake, and Jules' studies were a distant memory. They ended up at a swimming hole, and they both jumped in and swam until it was dark. They climbed out of the water and were drying off with a picnic blanket that Sheila always had stashed in the bike's luggage rack when a searchlight blinded them.

"What are you two doing out here by yourselves?" asked a sweaty cop from his patrol car.

"We just went for a swim, officer," said Sheila.

"Alone?"

"Yes. We go to university in Philly, and we're taking a break from finals."

"College girls, huh," said the creepy-looking cop.

"Yes, sir."

"Well, you know we have a curfew out here?"

"Oh, we didn't know that," lied Sheila.

Jules was scared but also irked because she knew the curfew didn't start until ten at night.

"It's not even seven yet," said Jules.

"And that's too late for two pretty young ladies like yourself to be out here."

"That's a good point, sir," said Sheila, who then leaned back and whispered to Jules, "Hold on."

Jules grabbed Sheila's waist as her friend kicked the bike into gear and peeled out so quickly that the back tires spat gravel onto the cop's windshield. The Triumph was so fast that Sheila and Jules were back at school within half an hour, pretty sure that the cop never even tried to pursue them.

JANUARY 9, 2017

Jules laughed at how obtuse everyone was back then but quickly put the brakes on her trip down memory lane. She had had an idea in the middle of the night and needed to talk to Richie as soon as possible. As she drove up his long gravel driveway, the gray light of the morning sun revealed the beauty of Richie's barn. She got out of the Ford and hurried past the stain-soaked wood, patched roof, and polished old hardware on the doors. Even though Jules had walked his property countless times, she couldn't help but stop that cold January morning and notice that every detail of the barn highlighted not only the passing of time but the love and dedication of its owner.

Richie had inherited the property from his parents, who had inherited it from theirs. Back in the day, there were chicken coops, dairy cows, pig pens, and even a few sheep roaming around. Jules fondly remembered the day she came over with eighteen-month-old Gina. As she and Richie sat out back talking, a crawling Gina suddenly pulled herself up on a rusted green combine and took her first steps into the cornfield.

Back then, Richie kept the farm up and running with military precision. Jules knew his dedication to the land was based on loyalty and respect for his mom and dad, both of whom Jules loved very much, and both of whom died—within a week of each other—back in 1975. The death of his parents at such a young age strengthened Richie's desire to hold on to their beloved farm, but Richie also took pride in being a farmer because, as he loved to tell Jules and Johnny, it was the perfect lifestyle. He woke up early and worked hard, outside, and with his hands. The best part, to Richie, was that he was beholden to no one besides the animals and the land. His ex-wife, Kay, however, did not see it the same way.

Jules was there the night that Richie and Kay met. She and Johnny had invited Richie to the Acorn Pub to have a drink to celebrate Jules' twenty-fourth birthday. After a few, Jules started talking about how hard it was to be a mom. Gina was only three at the time, but she had severe tantrums, and Jules was at her wits' end. Out of nowhere, the bartender said, "I'd rather have Syphilis than have kids."

The comment took Johnny and Jules aback, but Richie howled with laughter. None of them had ever met the bartender before, but it turned out that Hank—the grizzled old curmudgeon who owned the place and was the regular barkeep—had fallen sick, so his daughter, Kay, had covered his shift. As the night progressed, it became clear to Jules that Richie was smitten. Jules also warmed up to Kay, who was gregarious and funny. But Jules couldn't help but notice that Kay and Richie were complete opposites. Richie had always talked about wanting a big family and raising them in Warrensburg. Kay dreamed about moving up to New York and pursuing a career in advertising.

At the end of the day, neither got what they wanted from the other. To be fair to Kay, Jules knew that she didn't want kids because her parents were rough, and she wanted no part in ruining someone else's life. And to be fair to Richie, he loved to travel and see the world, but he didn't want to live anywhere besides Warrensburg.

Jules often thought that if Richie and Kay had lived somewhere else or in a different time, they probably would have divorced earlier, but they stuck it out for close to thirty years. The day Kay told Richie she was leaving because she had met someone else, Richie sat on Johnny and Jules' couch and said that he felt nothing but relief. Ironically, it wasn't long after Kay left that Richie sold the animals, cornfields, and farm equipment. He kept the barn and the house, but he was just about retired by the time he was fifty.

Jules was jealous of Richie's full life. He had always been good with investments, and the money he made from selling his land and equipment gave him a pretty good safety net to spend his days doing what he called the "simple things." But once a farmer, always a farmer, and Richie still woke up at five in the morning every day. But instead of milking the cows and gathering the eggs, Richie spent most of his early mornings walking through the woods. He loved fishing the Delaware, hiking at Hawk Mountain Conservatory, and visiting his backyard garden. Richie also loved to paint. He started with watercolors but, over the years, switched to oil painting exclusively and had a makeshift studio behind the barn. And that's where Jules found him that morning, stretching a new canvas.

Richie looked surprised to see Jules.

"Jules? Is everything okay?"

"Yeah, yeah, sorry. Everything is fine. But I need to talk to you privately about something, and I didn't want to do it on the phone."

Richie stood up. "Okay. Hit me."

"Well, without going into great detail. Johnny and I are going to kill the President-elect."

At first, Richie smirked, probably assuming it was a joke. But when he looked into Jules' eyes, she stared back with firm determination. He saw that Jules was completely serious, and his grin grew even more prominent.

"You crazy son of a bitch."

"Anyway. I thought you'd want to know," said Jules.

"Of course. And if I can help in any way . . ."

That was exactly what she wanted to hear.

"It's funny you should say that."

Jules explained to him that they needed a place for Johnny to take target practice.

"We need a place he could set up the exact shot. A mockup, day of scenario," said Jules.

"I can do that," replied Richie.

"That's what I thought, given your artistic talents," said Jules.

"Give me two or three days," said Richie.

"Oh, and FYI, I haven't told Johnny I'm enlisting your help."

"Why's that?" asked Richie.

"Because he thinks I've lost my marbles. And, I mean, in the grump's defense, it is a crazy idea."

"Those are usually the best kind."

"That's what I say. But I still need to work out some logistical stuff before Johnny is fully on board. I figured he could take some target practice over at your barn. It'll get him feeling good about himself. Plus, it'll get him out of my hair and give me some time to work out the details of how we get away with it."

"What kind of logistical stuff?"

"For one, my escape plan involves riding a motorcycle, and I haven't done that since Nixon was president."

"Ah."

"Plus, I accidentally got Becca involved. Not to mention, Gina is breathing down our necks, and a security guard at the hotel has already caught us scoping the joint out."

"Is that all?" joked Richie.

"Yeah, I think that's it."

"So, what is your plan as of now?" asked Richie.

"The plan is that we know he will be in Philly on the twenty-sixth, and we have a kid who got us access to the hotel across the street. It's only three stories up and not that far of a shot, so that shouldn't be the problem."

"Wait, that's *not* a problem?"

"I mean, practically speaking, it won't be hard for Johnny to make that shot once he gets his confidence back. The hard part is getting out of the hotel and getting away with it. Johnny's stuck on the 'how' part. Without an exit strategy, he's not going to do it."

"The way I see it, it's not about figuring out how to get away with it but how to get away *from* it."

"What do you mean?"

"The way the world is with cameras and phones everywhere, you can't do this and expect they won't know you did it. So, you have to figure out how to escape and, even more importantly, stay hidden after the fact."

"Ah," said Jules, half agreeing.

Then Richie added, "And if you wanna get Johnny to do something, make it simple. Come up with a ten-point plan."

"Interesting," said Jules.

"The man loves ten-point plans."

That was true. Johnny even had a ten-point plan for how to make a good ten-point plan.

"Well, either way, give me the details of where you're going to do it and which day. And I'll set something up in my barn that looks and feels like the real thing," added Richie.

"Oh my God, you're so great. Thank you. I'll text you."

"You're welcome, but I'd rather you not text me the details of the crime we're about to commit together."

"Right. Right. I'll jot them down and bring them over tomorrow morning."

"Great."

That night, before falling asleep, Jules devised a ten-point plan.

CHAPTER 13

JANUARY 12, 2017

HOLY CRAP, IT'S FREEZING.

Johnny got out of the pickup and rubbed his hands together. Besides thinking about the cold, Johnny was preoccupied with how mad he had been when Jules told him the night before that Richie was now involved in her hare-brained scheme. Johnny was hoping the scope of the insanity would shrink, not grow.

Richie walked out of his house and met Johnny at the truck. It was so cold they could see their breath as they talked.

"Morning."

"Morning. Sorry, she roped you into this nonsense."

"Please. As I told your better half, I am happy to be part of this historic endeavor."

"I swear to God. I don't know what to do with her right now. She has this nutty idea stuck in her head, and I honestly do not know what to do or say to stop her."

"I hear you. But I also remember what a monster he was. Is."

"Yeah."

Jesus Christ. Is he as crazy as she is?

"Maybe there is a—" Richie stopped when he saw Gina's SUV pull into his driveway.

She was coming to drop off Becca so that Jules could have some time at the house to herself. She had told Johnny it was so she could clean, but he knew that having Becca spend the day with him and Richie was just another chess move in Jules' crazy murder game.

The Toyota rolled up, and Gina and Becca got out.

"Oh my God, it's so cold," said Gina.

"Thirty-six, according to Channel Four," said Richie.

"Well, it feels negative thirty-six."

Johnny turned to Becca, who had yet to say a word. "Morning, sweetie."

Becca just yawned. Gina rolled her eyes and said to Richie, "You must forgive my daughter. She's not a morning person."

"Teenagers are nocturnal by nature," Richie smiled.

Gina turned to Johnny, "And why are you out here so early anyway?"

"Richie is letting me use his barn for some work," lied Johnny, looking back at Richie. The two old friends made eye contact, and Richie nodded, implying he understood not to say anything to Gina about what they were really up to.

"Work?" asked Gina.

Johnny lied again, "I'm finally refinishing your mother's coffee table."

"Oh! Can I see?" asked an excited Gina as she walked toward the barn.

Richie immediately stepped in front of her and said, "You don't want to go in there."

"Why not?"

Richie, who was not a good liar, looked stuck. Johnny stepped up. "Dead skunk. Nasty."

Gina cringed. "Ew. Okay. Well, you three have fun."

Johnny kissed her, Richie waved goodbye, and Becca yawned again.

After Gina drove off, Johnny and Richie looked at each other like they had just gotten away with something. Without saying a word, they led Becca to the barn, and Richie and Johnny rolled back the enormous sliding doors.

Holy crap. Richie did it.

I mean, if this weren't such a crazy thing, it would be a beautiful thing.

Inside the barn was a mock setup of the Presidential motorcade. Two-by-fours propped up painted life-like images on wood cut-outs. Secret service agents surrounded a limo, motorcycles escorted SUVs, rope lines kept spectators back, and wooden reporters snapped photos. Behind the motorcade was a giant mural of the Madison Philadelphia Hotel's back entrance. The centerpiece was a wooden President next to a replica of his Whitehouse Chief Strategist. Behind them stood a wooden Vice President that looked more alive than the real VP. All the building facades were so enormous and exact that Nina and Johnny couldn't help but be blown away by the attention to detail and scope. Richie had painted everything from the limo windshields to the crowds of people with such exactness and authenticity that even the low winter sun's shadows had been made to replicate how it would appear through the alleyway at the time of the President's arrival. Johnny scanned the room and saw a drill, a jigsaw, a table saw, hammers, nails, boxes of nuts and bolts, piles of sawdust, and half-empty paint cans scattered to the side. Half a dozen four-by-eight sheets of plywood and more paint cans were in the corner.

Becca spoke first, "This is balls-out, Uncle Richie."

Richie beamed with pride. "Well, I'm not sure I'd use those exact words. But I thought if you lunatics are really gonna do this, you need to get it right. I also set up a mock window three stories up and a tree at roughly the same distance and angle as the two hotels."

Johnny struck a match, lit a cigar, and simply said, "Unbelievable. My crazy wife got you to do all this."

"It was my pleasure."

"I mean, it's only been three days."

"Luckily, Home Depot delivers."

"You must've broken your back."

"Please. I liked doing it. Felt good to have a project," said Richie.

"The detail . . . okay. But tell me you're not as crazy as she is?"

"What do you mean?"

"What do I mean?! I mean, I think she might believe we're going to do this. But you have to know that we're not, right?"

"I guess."

"Not 'I guess.' There's no way we're going to do this." Johnny looked over at Becca and made eye contact before adding, "And this goes for you, too. We are not doing this. Your grandmother is going through something, and that's okay. She's allowed. But this, this is a delusion."

Becca rolled her eyes and said, "Whatever."

Johnny had no idea what to do with that "whatever," but the way he figured, Becca was a kid and had no idea about anything. Richie, however, ought to know better. He turned back to his old friend, "There is no way we are going to kill a man."

"No. I don't imagine you are."

"Good. Because you're the self-proclaimed pacifist, so when the time comes, and Jules and I have this conversation, I will need you to back me up."

"Sure. But for now, what's the harm in humoring her?"

"That's why I'm going along with it. Although the longer this goes on, the more harm there may be in it."

"Harm is relative."

"See that hippy-dippy way of speaking makes me question your sanity too."

Richie laughed.

"That being said, I do enjoy some target practice," added Johnny.

Moments later, he retrieved his rifle case from his passenger seat and headed to a tree on the other side of the property. At the tree, he looked up and saw a deer stand in the high branches with a window frame like the one in the hotel nailed in front of it.

"Richie, you goddamn nut job," said Johnny, smiling to himself.

As he climbed the rope ladder to the window set-up, Johnny favored his left hand because the right one bothered him. The climb was high, and the endeavor left Johnny winded.

Johnny took five minutes to catch his breath, assembled the Winchester, and readied his shot. Through the branches, he could see

Richie and Becca sitting in Adirondack chairs fifty yards away. Johnny smiled when he saw that they were both covered in blankets and drinking out of a thermos that Johnny assumed was full of Richie's famous hot chocolate.

Eventually, Richie yelled out, "Anytime you're ready, Johnny."

Johnny got focused. He breathed.

"Pappi. Hello? We're waiting!" shouted Becca.

Johnny was silent. He listened to the wind.

Richie and Becca laughed a bit, and then Richie yelled, "EARTH TO JOHNNY…BRAVO, BRAVO, KINGFISH. THIS IS DELTA LEADER."

Johnny tuned it all out. The world went silent. All he heard was the beating of his own heart and the air slowly filling his lungs.

Inside the barn, two gunshots ripped through a wooden reporter's chest. He had missed.

Just like Ed's windshield.

He took a second deep breath, readied his shot, and fired again.

This time, it hit the wooden Vice President. Closer, but still off.

Shit.

CHAPTER 14

WHILE JOHNNY, RICHIE, AND BECCA were at Richie's barn, Jules was in her garage, facing a big black tarp, paralyzed with fear. Sheila's old '65 blue and black Triumph Bonneville was under the cover. Jules felt confident it would run, but not that she could ride it. She hadn't even looked at the bike in over forty years. To Jules, the classic motorcycle was still Sheila's.

I have no right to it.

There was also the shooting pain in her leg and butt from sliding down the laundry chute. It had only been three days since the stitches had dissolved.

But for Jules' caper to work, she and Becca had to be proficient in hotwiring.

Deep breath. Focus.

She repeated the ten-point plan she had devised while lying next to snoring Johnny the night before.

Step one: Practice sliding down the chute. Check.

Step two: Hide the rifle. Check.

Step three: Watch DIY hotwiring videos on YouTube. Check.

Step four: Practice ride on the Triumph. *Working on it.*

Step five: Practice hotwiring on a random bike to ensure we can do it.

Step six: Do a run-through of the escape route on the Triumph.

Step seven: Get the rifle back in the hotel.
Step eight: Get disguises.
Step nine: Kill the Dummy.
Step ten: Escape.

Jules ripped the tarp off, wheeled the bike outside, and hopped on.

So many memories. So many feelings. Shit, not now.

There was no time for nostalgia. She turned the key, pumped, primed, released the clutch, and kicked, and then the engine howled.

At first, getting her balance was tricky, but it all came back when she turned out of the driveway. Just like riding a bike. Literally.

On those country roads, Jules opened the Triumph up. She enjoyed the wind in her hair and the sun on her cheeks. She didn't even remember this sense of joy enough to know she missed it. *This is what freedom feels like.*

———

Later that night, Jules was in bed reading *Cooking Light* magazine when Johnny walked in from the bathroom, still in the middle of brushing his teeth.

"Did you lock the front door?" he asked.

"Sure did," she replied without looking up from her article.

"Thanks."

With his toothbrush still in his mouth, Johnny stood there looking at his wife for a full minute. Eventually, she acknowledged his prolonged gaze.

"What?"

"You look nice right now."

"Oh, shush."

"No, I mean it. Your hair, I mean, everything. You look nice."

"Thanks."

"And dinner was great."

Jules put the magazine down and looked at Johnny suspiciously. "What's going on?"

"Nothing."

They both smiled flirtatiously, and then Johnny started brushing again before he walked back into the bathroom, chuckling like a kid. It was a small thing, but to Jules, it felt enormous. Johnny hadn't looked at her like that or flirted with her in years, maybe decades.

JANUARY 13, 2017

After Becca got out of school, Jules gave her a quick riding lesson. It didn't go well. The bike was too heavy, and she had a teenager's attention span. But despite laying the bike down on the driveway three times, Becca managed to ride successfully up and down Willard Place, and Jules decided to call it a day.

"That's it?" asked Becca.

"That's it," replied Jules.

"But how am I going to be able to ride it to the hotel?"

Jules had no intention of letting Becca actually participate in her plan.

"We can practice another day, but that's enough for today. Don't always be such an overachiever, and have a little patience."

Becca sulked, but Jules cheered her up with an ice cream cone at Robertson's Family Creamery. After dropping Becca off at Gina's, Jules went shopping for supplies. She picked up some climbing equipment from REI and some motorcycle gear from the Harley-Davidson store on Route 15. She used cash from an ATM, so it was untraceable, and covered her face with her hands when walking by the store's CC cameras. It was adventurous. Jules felt like a character in one of those British cop shows she loved to watch on Netflix.

Killer Grandma, at your disposal.

JANUARY 14, 2017

The following day, Jules picked Becca up at school in the Ford and drove to a neighboring town to try their hotwiring skills. Parked on a quiet street, Jules grabbed two new black helmets and two pairs of black gloves from the truck's bed. She handed one set to Becca and told her to put them on. They walked silently for a few blocks until they reached an industrial part of town. Jules gestured to a bike parked up the road.

"I saw this parked here last Friday, and it was here for eight straight hours. The guy who owns it works in the big building across the street, so it should be safe to practice on as long as we get it back by five."

"Wait, you sat here and watched this bike all day?"

"Every good heist starts with casing the joint."

Becca laughed and then said, "Cool."

"So, where did you tell your mother you would be right now?"

"I told her I was studying with a friend after school."

"And she believed you?"

"Good thing about being a geek: everyone believes me."

Jules and Becca left the pickup and walked over to the parked bike. Jules took out a screwdriver, wire cutter, and chisel from her purse.

"Shouldn't I be the one practicing since I'll be doing it on the day of the . . . thing?" asked Becca.

Becca's hesitation to use the word "murder" embarrassed Jules. She knew involving her granddaughter in the plot was an irresponsible mistake, and she was anxious to get her out of the loop.

It won't be long now.

"You can try another day, but I think it's best if I try it the first time," lied Jules.

"If you say so," said Becca, disappointed.

Jules tried to change the subject.

"So why did you call yourself a geek before?"

"What?"

"You said the good thing about being a geek is that everyone believes you," said Jules.

"Oh yeah. I mean, I know that I'm smart and that's the way every-one sees me."

"When I was your age, I was a good student, too. It's nothing to be ashamed of."

"I'm not. I love who I am."

"Those are the best five words I have ever heard. 'I love who I am.'"

Jules then turned her attention to the bike's handlebars. She slammed the screwdriver into the ignition, popped off the key lock, pulled two wires, stripped the ends, and twirled them together.

"Yeah. This bitch is actualized," said Becca.

Jules laughed. "I have to say. When I was your age, I had much more fear than you, the same amount of smarts, but none of your confidence. Good for you."

And with that, Jules got on, kicked the start, and revved the engine.

They high-fived, and then Becca climbed on the bike and wrapped her arms around her grandmother, and they took off.

It was a short ride through the town, but it felt thrilling. Jules missed the feel of the wind on her face and the bike's weight between her legs. There was something exhilarating about shifting her weight as she rounded the big curve by the credit union. Speeding out of the turn, Jules felt simultaneously aware of the danger and how natural it felt. Even more exciting was the fact that she had just stolen something. It was the second time in Jules' life that she had knowingly committed a crime. As Becca squeezed Jules' waist, they giggled like they were in on some private joke. Jules thought, *What a miraculously strange life*.

When they pulled onto Main Street, Becca yelled, "You and Pappi are crazy! I love it!" And with that declaration, the bliss Jules felt gave way to anxiety. She knew that Johnny still thought the entire endeavor was a fool's errand and that he had been humoring her and "just having fun." She knew he still didn't think they would go through with it. He wasn't wrong to think it was insane for two senior citizens to shoot and kill another senior citizen who happened to be president and believe they could get away with it. It was stupid.

Personally, Jules didn't care if they got caught. She thought it was worth it. She remembered one of the crime books that Johnny liked to listen to when he drove—a story about a retired cop who became a public defender. The publisher had the arrogance to write on the thriller's CD case, "Not since Atticus Finch has there been a literary character with such respect for the law." The main character had been on both sides of the law and, above all, honored the legal system's process. One night, a burglar broke into his house while he was sleeping. After a series of unrealistic plot devices, his entire family was tragically murdered, and the killer was arrested. At the trial, the protagonist snatched the bailiff's gun, killed the bad guy, and avenged his family. Even though Jules thought the story was a bit contrived and silly, she remembered the character's speech after his sentencing to life in prison: "I accept my fate. I had to kill that guy for what he did to my family, but I respect the legal system enough to know that I deserve to go to jail. It's a fair price that I pay willingly and honorably."

Jules liked that sentiment. She felt the same about killing the asshole; she was willing to pay the price. She knew she had to kill him, that he deserved to be dead, and doing so would be just and righteous. But she also respected that it was against the law and that people shouldn't take things into their own hands. In theory, Jules believed murder should be against the law, no matter the reason—that a person who took another person's life should, without exception, go to jail. In her heart, she knew that if her plan succeeded, they should be sent away. Even though it was moral and, in her mind, ethical, it was still illegal. However, her sense of justice was conflicted because she knew that Johnny did not feel the same way. Johnny would only go through with it if she could convince him that her plan was solid. But Jules knew it was impossible to get away with it. Maybe Richie's distinction of getting away from it was a better way to look at it.

As she pulled the bike back into the same spot where they had stolen it less than an hour before, Jules decided to solve that puzzle another day. Instead, she was going to enjoy the moment.

She parked, separated the wires she had tied together to hotwire the bike, put back the key lock, and walked away—no need to trouble the owner. Except for an emptier gas tank, the owner wouldn't even notice the bike had been borrowed.

"That was fun!" said Becca.

Jules loved her granddaughter's playfulness. "It was! Okay, stealing a motorcycle, check. Now we need to see if our escape route is up to snuff."

They drove the pickup back home and hopped on the Triumph.

An hour later, they were in Philadelphia, and Jules parked the bike behind the Marriott Hotel and hopped off.

"Follow me."

Becca and Jules walked over to the employee's entrance on the right side of the building.

"Okay. So, we'll exit here after your grandpa and I leave the laundry chute."

"And if all goes well, the bike will be there waiting for you," said Becca.

"I still don't think you should be the one stealing it," said Jules.

"We talked about this already. You agreed that it's the smart move."

"Yeah. I guess."

That was all Jules needed to hear. The fact that Becca was so committed to being involved convinced Jules that she wouldn't be. She had already put everything in motion and knew that Becca would no longer be part of it by night's end. Jules hated lying to her granddaughter, but it was the lesser of two evils.

Oblivious, Becca started jogging over to the bike, and Jules followed.

"So, you and Pappi come out of the hotel, hop on the bike, and—"

They got on the bike and put their helmets back on.

"And we're . . ." Jules checked her watch, "off!"

It was the magic hour as the two ladies weaved down country roads, laughing out loud the entire time. They turned onto a small dirt path that brought them to an exposed underground storm drain system. They couldn't suppress their laughter and cheers as they rode through the massive, dark pipe.

When they finally came to a stop, Becca hugged her grandma. Jules checked her watch and made a mental note that it only took thirty-seven minutes to go from the Marriott to the manhole cover above her.

"That wasn't that bad," said Jules.

"Not at all," said Becca, adding, "But where are we?"

"You'll find out in one second. On the actual day of the shooting, your grandfather and I will do that same drive, leave our helmets and jackets in here, and then change into a yellow windbreaker and climb these stairs."

Jules gestured to an industrial ladder leading up the wall to the street above them. As they climbed, Jules said, "Our car, with fake plates, will be up here. I already made sure there are no cameras on the country roads back to our place, so we should be safe."

Above ground, the manhole opened, and Jules and Becca climbed out. Jules bent down and pushed the cover back.

"You're pretty strong for an old chick," said Becca.

Jules flexed a muscle and grinned but then held up a crowbar, "It's all leverage. I would think that someone as smart as—"

Jules stopped mid-sentence when she saw Gina. Her daughter was pissed.

"Shit," said Becca.

CHAPTER 15

JOHNNY WAS READING UPSTAIRS WHEN he heard his front door swing open. Then he heard the commotion in the living room.

What now?

He walked downstairs and found Jules, Gina, and Becca in the kitchen. The three ladies were clearly pissed off at each other.

Johnny grabbed some leftover chicken cutlets out of the fridge. He sat as Gina paced—stove, refrigerator, sink, stove, refrigerator, sink—and then proceeded to eat.

"I think it's time we consider moving you two somewhere more supportive," said Gina.

"Supportive? What the hell does that mean?"

"It means she wants to put you two in a home," said Becca.

Johnny and Jules exchanged a solemn look. Then they burst out laughing.

"Please," said Johnny.

"I would love it. Someone to make the meals and clean. And all those planned activities. Ah, delightful!" said Jules.

"Sounds like a vacation. But, Sweetie, can you afford that?" Johnny smirked at his daughter.

Becca laughed, and Gina snapped at her, "This is NOT funny."

Johnny stood up, "I agree. It's not funny being lectured by my daughter."

He wasn't sure what Jules had been up to, but he sure as hell did not like being talked to like a child. Jules told him a few nights earlier that her plan included escaping through the drainage pipes and that somehow it would lead to getting Becca uninvolved, but he only half listened to what Jules said. Johnny was an expert at tuning people out.

"Honey. We're just having fun. Becca spends so much time studying and working so hard, she needs some relaxation," said Jules.

"She ain't wrong. I hate to say this, but you helicopter her," added Johnny while making a helicopter noise by hitting his hands on his chest.

"Nanna and Pappi are only—"

"I don't even want to hear one single word from you right now." Gina turned her anger back on her parents. "And if you two think this will be like the conversation we had when you took Becca on horseback when she was three without asking us, you're dead wrong. Why the hell were you riding a motorcycle through the sewer?!"

No one had a good response to that.

"The only thing more insane than having to ask that question is that you three don't have an answer."

"Well, for the record, it's not a sewer. It's a runoff drain. Slight difference," said Johnny.

There was another quiet beat before Gina turned to Becca, "You. In the car. NOW."

Becca stormed out, followed by Gina.

After the car drove off, Jules took their plates to the sink.

"That went well."

"Only you would think that went well," said Johnny.

"It's for the best."

"How'd you get Gina there to catch you two?" asked Johnny.

"I texted her, making it look like I intended to send it to Becca. It said, 'Honey. Please meet us at Crossman and 3rd in Munsonville at 7:00 p.m. We'll be by the pothole. Don't tell your mom. She would be so mad if she knew what we were up to.'"

"Smart."

"It should be easier now, knowing that Becca's out of it and pro-
tected."

"Easy?"

"As easy as you making the shot."

Johnny figured that Richie or Becca—or both—would have ratted
him out and told Jules that he had missed the first five shots he took
before hitting his mark. And he knew she was using his feeling of
inadequacy against him. But knowing that didn't make it less effective.
Calling him out shut him down.

"Agreed," said a somewhat defeated Johnny.

Johnny grabbed a cookie from a plate on the table but dropped it
when he felt a shooting pain in his hand.

JANUARY 16, 2017

Getting out of bed on Monday morning was hard. The pain in Johnny's hand was that excruciating. Just pushing down on the soft mat-
tress to stand was unbearable.

Suck it up. It will heal on its own.

After finishing breakfast, Jules told Johnny to wait for a second,
got up, and went upstairs. She came back down with two big brown
shopping bags.

"What's in that?" asked Johnny.

"Our costumes."

"What?"

"Our disguises so that we can check into the hotel today."

*Well, I guess this is the point of no return. Somebody needs to start
talking sense.*

Johnny stood up, determined to confront her. But Jules pulled out
a long, brown, wavy wig; round, wire-rimmed purple sunglasses; and
a white sweatshirt that said "NEW YORK CITY" across the chest.
The outfit was reminiscent of the iconic Bob Gruen photo of John
Lennon hanging upstairs in Johnny's office.

"I thought this might appeal to you," said Jules proudly.

Seeing the shirt and glasses hit like a brick.

━━━━━

JULY 1972

After Johnny's fourth beer, Richie played Lennon's first post-Beatles solo album.

What is this crap?

They were sitting in Richie's kitchen, and as was often the case back then, Johnny was annoyed with his old friend. Richie was in full hippie mode, and he and Johnny disagreed about everything happening in the country. They could not see eye to eye, whether about something substantial like politics or more inane like music.

Johnny had never been a huge rock fan and was more into crooners, like Eddie Fisher, Bobby Darin, and Sinatra. Even in Vietnam, his platoon listened to classical pieces rather than the contemporary rock that was more beloved by other sailors and soldiers.

As he sat at his friend's small kitchen table, recklessly day-drinking, he could feel himself start to unravel. Like so many people, Johnny was a mess after returning from Vietnam. Re-entry into a post-war society left him emotionally, physically, and spiritually defeated.

Rather than argue with Richie, he surrendered, sat back, and shut his mouth. He could not have been less prepared for the impact the music would have on him. Something about the *John Lennon/Plastic Ono Band* album, specifically the song "God," profoundly affected him.

Johnny had gone to war as a Catholic. His father and mother were Catholic, and their parents were Catholic. The idea of not being part of the church or believing was never an option for Johnny, but being in the war changed his mind about religion. He used to joke that the cliche that there are no atheists in foxholes was the opposite of the truth. Johnny said that a foxhole is the one place where no one should believe in God because the only all-powerful thing in war is a bullet or a bomb. But it wasn't just what Johnny saw and did that made him lose faith. It was also being around different people and being exposed to other cultures and beliefs. It didn't seem logical to Johnny that with all the gods in the world, he was following the right one because of who he was and where he was born.

At home, he struggled with his newfound atheism because, suddenly, he was surrounded by believers again. Johnny's parents were still alive and attending church, but Jules' sudden faith freaked him out the most. Jules was raised Protestant, but when Johnny went to war, she sought comfort at his parents' Catholic church and, over time, made the leap and converted. Johnny always suspected that becoming a Catholic was less about her beliefs and more about giving the middle finger to her own parents. Either way, Jules went to church every Sunday while Johnny was deployed and even had Gina baptized and confirmed.

It wasn't just religion that no longer made sense—it was everything. His perspective of the world and sense of self had been flipped upside down. Then Johnny heard that Lennon song, "God," and he had an insight. Like the young rock star from Liverpool, who sang, "The dream was over," and that he had relinquished his beliefs in everything, including his former rock band, Johnny, too, felt the dream was over. When the song ended with, "I just believe in me. Yoko and me. That's reality," Johnny felt an inkling of peace. For days afterward, he meditated on that idea—that the world at large was insignificant compared to the love and connection shared with family. It became clear to Johnny that all that mattered was his wife and daughter. Johnny knew that Jules and Gina loved him and that he loved them. For Johnny Coletti, that was all there was. He wrapped his arms around the simplicity of family. He let go of everything else and focused on that and that alone for the rest of his life.

JANUARY 16, 2017

Standing in his kitchen, Johnny slipped on the sweatshirt and looked at his wife. Jules was holding the wig and the sunglasses with a look that said, "Come on, you know you want to." And Johnny did want to.

Forgetting about the confrontation and the whack-a-doodle murderous aspirations of his wife, Johnny made his way into the bathroom to look at himself in the mirror. Because of his age and size, he didn't look anything like John Lennon. He looked more like John Goodman. Also, neither the font nor the red coloring of the "New York City" print would make anyone else think of the John Lennon photo. But he loved it. When he came out of the bathroom, he found Jules wearing a black jacket and a white t-shirt, and her long gray hair was pulled up into a beret.

"Who are you supposed to be?"

"I'm Samuel L. Jackson, mother-fucker," said Jules.

"Jesus Christ."

CHAPTER 16

THE DRIVE IN THE TRUCK to the Marriott was sublime.

The John Lennon costume was a stroke of genius! I think he is starting to enjoy this!

They met Jordan by the employee entrance, unloaded the lamp (with the rifle inside) into the laundry bin, drove a few blocks away, and parked on a quiet, residential street.

Jules could not have been happier as they walked back to the hotel in costume and met Jordan at the concierge desk. That joy was quickly erased when Jordan said, a bit too loudly, "Nice costumes, Mr. and Mrs. Coletti!"

"Sam and Pam Smith, checking in, please."

"Oh, yeah. Sorry about that," whispered Jordan.

"How do you find your way home after work?" asked Johnny, sarcastically.

"I don't get it," replied Jordan. He then turned to Jules, "We need a credit card for incidentals."

Jules froze. She hadn't thought about payment.

I'm an idiot.

She handed Jordan her credit card, and out of the corner of her eye, she saw Pags on his stool, staring right at them. The first time she saw him, Jules thought Pags was nothing more than a lazy rent-a-cop, but now she could see that he was more than that. He, too, was like a character from one of Johnny's books. She could almost hear one of those manly authors describing Pag as a guy who looked soft on the outside, but inside, that hard-ass-cop fire still burned in his belly.

Jules watched as Pags took a small, leather-covered flip pad from his back pocket and jotted some notes. *What the hell is he writing?*

Jules avoided looking at him as she and Johnny walked across the lobby and got into the elevator. *Screw him, stick to the ten-point plan.*

On the third floor, Jordan walked them down the hallway to the same room they had visited the week before, which he had kept unoccupied until they arrived. Jules was happy to see that the oversized laundry bin was in front of their door. Johnny did not seem to share in her pleasure.

"You left this here?" asked Johnny.

"Yuppers," said a gleeful Jordan.

"With a rifle inside? What if someone else had moved it?" asked an incredulous Johnny.

Didn't think of that.

Jules reached into the bin and fished around until she pulled out the green lamp.

"Wow. Every time I'm convinced this can't get more absurd or insane, it does."

They walked into the room, and Jules crossed to the nightstand and put the lamp back.

"Good as new."

Jordan looked pleasantly surprised by Jules' craftsmanship. "Whoa. That actually looks great."

"No one noticed the missing lamp the past few days?" asked Johnny.

"Nope."

Johnny said nothing and just stared at him.

"Okay then. Well, I guess you guys have the room for the next nine days, so I'll leave you two to it."

"Thank you."

"Yeah, thanks, Skippy."

"Okay, then. It's Jordan. But either way, okay."

After Jordan left, Jules let out a sigh of relief.

Since we have to wait until that guy Pags' shift ends and he goes home to do another run-through, I am going to try out that fancy bathtub. I'm sure Johnny will be more than happy to have a few minutes alone to read.

She kissed him on the cheek and went to take a bath.

NOVEMBER 6, 1968

In her parents' house, Jules walked upstairs, went into the bathroom, and locked the door. She had been trying all day not to cry, especially in front of her mom, but she couldn't hold it in any longer.

She ran a bath, stripped off her clothes, and fell into the warm water. Her mind was racing with so many thoughts, but she couldn't shake the question of what Sheila had done.

Did she overdose by accident?

Or on purpose?

Could she actually do that?

Why didn't she call Jules?

She must have felt so sad and alone.

The helplessness Jules felt about her friend was paralyzing. The realization that Sheila was in so much pain but couldn't talk to Jules shook her foundation. Maybe their friendship was more one-sided than Jules thought. Logically, Jules knew that wasn't true. She knew that the pain Sheila felt was overwhelming and that her death had nothing to do with Jules or the legitimacy of their friendship. She knew that the trauma was the fault of only one person.

It was a sadness Jules didn't have the tools to deal with, and being around her mom only made matters worse. It reminded Jules that, besides Johnny, Sheila was the only person who had ever shown her any empathy or kindness. She wanted to call Sheila to talk about the pain she was feeling. That irony was too much for Jules to handle.

After her bath, Jules went downstairs where her mom had made a roasted chicken dinner. Her dad was sitting at the table, reading the newspaper. She had been expecting him to pick her up, but it was her mom who showed up at the terminal. They gave no explanation, but Jules assumed he told his wife to do it, and she acquiesced without a word.

Even though Jules hadn't seen or talked to her father in months, the man didn't even look up from the article he was reading.

"Hi, Dad."

"How was the bus ride?"

"It was fine."

"Good, good."

And that was it. There was silence for a long time until Jules said, "Can you pass me the potatoes?"

"No," said her mom.

"What do you mean, no?" asked Jules.

"I mean, you look like you put on a little weight at school. You need to ease up on the starches."

Jules felt embarrassed. She had put on some weight, but still, what the hell?

"Well, you'll be happy to know that I don't think I'm going back."

"Back?"

"To school."

"Oh," was all her mom said.

Jules wanted to scream. She wanted her mom to ask why so that she could tell her that she felt scared and crippled. Jules wanted her mom to cry with her and hug her. She wanted her dad to protect her and tell her that she should finish school, that she had worked so hard to get where she was and was so close to accomplishing something monumental and vital. She wanted one of them to say they would protect her from that monster and do something about it. She wanted these two old people sitting at the table with her to love her as much as she loved them. She wanted to be a kid. She wanted support instead of shame; comfort instead of condemnation; direction instead of disappointment.

Jules opened her mouth, but the only thing that came out was the chicken and potatoes she threw up all over the white linen tablecloth.

JANUARY 16, 2017

Johnny and Jules walked down the hallway wearing black sweat suits, boots, and miner hats with lights. In their matching backpacks were a change of clothes and their disguises. Jules reached into her pocket and pulled out two pairs of gloves. She handed the larger pair to Johnny.

"The guy at REI said that these are the best slip-resistant rock-climbing gloves and boots they make. We can try to climb down instead of free-falling."

Putting on the gloves, Johnny said, "They feel great."

Jules climbed into the laundry chute much more purposefully than their last attempt. The chute was still dark, but she could see better this time because of the lights on their hats. Stretching out her arms and legs, she put pressure on the sides and eased her way to the ground floor. Johnny was right behind her.

"This is great!" said Jules with pride.

"Much better."

At the bottom, Johnny and Jules climbed out into the laundry room unscathed. She hugged him, and they removed their gear, which she put in Johnny's backpack. No one paid the two baby boomers any mind as they strolled through the employee entrance, down the stairs, and into the alley where Sheila's motorcycle was parked and waiting for them.

"It really does feel like we're invisible to everyone," said Jules.

"It's old people's superpower," said Johnny.

Johnny looked at the old Triumph and grinned. "It's nice to see Sheila's old bike up and running."

"Yeah, I agree. And even though I feel like it's okay to use for our run-through now, especially since Becca and I already proved that we can jack one when we need to, next time it should be—"

"Jack? Did you say 'jack?' You need to stop watching S.V.U." Johnny interrupted.

"Shush. I was just saying that leaving a stolen bike here all day would be risky. But without Becca helping anymore, I'm going to have to do it in the morning."

CHAPTER 17

JOHNNY COULD FEEL HIS HAND throbbing as he climbed behind Jules on the back of the bike. He was already shooting like crap, but with the increased agony, he had little faith he could hit a bale of hay, let alone a moving target. He contemplated telling Jules that his wrist had been bothering him for months and that inching down the chute had exacerbated the pain. But he chose not to fess up because he was actually happy for her. Jules' newfound passion for planning her caper brought something out in her that Johnny hadn't seen in decades. Her desire and excitement brought her back to life, which attracted him and brought him back to life as well.

Despite all the good feelings, a giant elephant remained in the room. Johnny knew in his heart that his wife thought they would go through with it. She had somehow convinced herself that two seventy-year-olds were going to shoot and kill another seventy-year-old—who also happened to be the President—steal a motorcycle, and drive off into the sunset. It was a fun fantasy to him but a reality to her. Johnny also knew that Jules had passed a point of no return. The hope that she would snap out of it on her own was gone. Therefore, Johnny had to be the one to break it to Jules that they couldn't go through with it. But when and how to do it in a firm and final way? At some point, sooner than later, he would need to shut this all down.

Whenever Johnny remembered the duality of his wife's reality, her enthusiasm and delusion, it forced him to see his wife as a raving lunatic. He knew if he broached the subject with her, she would feel deflated and hurt and mad and disappear back into her previous two-dimensional version of herself. The renaissance they were experiencing would turn to dust.

Fortunately, Johnny learned in the military, especially in a war, to compartmentalize his life. He often joked that he was happy to be the frog in the boiling water as long as he didn't know the water was boiling. What did he care? By the time he figured it out, he'd be dead. He was great at dealing with the harsh realities of life by ignoring them. He could accept whatever he could avoid. So, once again, Johnny ignored the fact that his wife was living in a fantasy and let it be.

Soon, but not today.

Instead, Johnny sat on that old Triumph Bonneville, wrapped his arms around Jules' waist, and started laughing. As his wife kickstarted the bike, he slid his hands up to her chest, and she blushed. It was provocative and ridiculous. Hell, it was romantic.

Suddenly, they were swerving in and out of traffic in a beautiful dance. Eventually, they reached the water pipe and drove in. They rode in the dark and silence for a little while until they stopped at the ladder. Without speaking, they got off the bike, removed their helmets and jackets, changed into their yellow windbreakers, and left everything else behind as they climbed the stairs.

They popped up through the manhole and walked to Johnny's truck, which was waiting for them. After they circled the Millpond, they returned to the sewer pipe, walked in, and retrieved Sheila's bike.

As they loaded it into the pickup bed, Jules said, "What do you say after we drop this off at home, we slip back into our disguises and head back to the hotel?"

"You mean for the night?"

"Why not?"

"Room service?"

"I love it!"

JANUARY 17, 2017

The following morning, Johnny sat in the hotel bed and surveyed the trashed room. An empty food platter and an ice bucket were on the floor. On the nightstand, next to the lamp with the hidden rifle, there were two empty Jack Daniel's bottles from the minibar and a lipstick-stained, half-empty glass of sparkling water.

What a night.

"What time is it?" asked Jules as she woke up.

"Who cares?" answered Johnny.

"Last night was so much fun," said Jules.

"Agreed. That was the most money we have spent on a meal in our forty-nine years together."

"And it was worth every penny. But I wasn't talking about the food."

"Oh. I have to be honest. I wasn't all the way sure that everything down there would even work properly anymore."

"Well, it worked fine," said Jules, adding, "I mean, it was better than fine."

"Fine, will do."

Johnny was in heaven. His head was clear, and he felt hope for the first time in years. Being intimate with his wife had removed a burden.

If it weren't for the fact that my wife has completely flipped her bird, things would be picture-perfect right now.

A few hours later, they left the hotel to return home dressed as Sam and Pam Smith.

It was a crisp, clear winter morning. When they returned home, Johnny made some coffee and started a fire. Johnny noticed they were low on wood, so he downed his cup of java and went outside to split some more logs. He stopped at the woodpile by the garage, grabbed a thick, round log, and placed it on a flattened circle of snow.

He rubbed his hands together and blew hot air onto them. Then he raised the axe and split the wood perfectly.

Upon making contact with the wood, Johnny recoiled in pain.

"Mother fuck!"

With tears in his eyes, he fell to the ground.

Jesus.

Eventually, he got up. The pain was like nothing he had ever felt, but Johnny would rather endure it than have Jules see him like that. He had just gotten his virility back, and, despite the psychological cliche of a rifle representing his manhood, not being able to use his shooting hand felt as emasculating as he could imagine.

He snuck inside, iced his wrist, and spent the rest of the morning avoiding Jules.

Late that afternoon, Johnny was at the table drinking a beer and reading when Jules walked in. She looked at the mostly empty firewood rack in the mudroom and said, "Thought you were gonna chop some wood?"

"Yeah. But I was so close to finishing my book, I figured we had enough for now. I can do more tomorrow."

Jules walked to the fridge, grabbed some chicken parts, and seasoned them in a pan. "I saw you through the window. It isn't the arthritis, is it?"

Jesus.

"I'm fine."

Jules came over to him, took his beer out of his left hand, and put it on the table.

"Pick it up with your other hand."

"Give me a break."

She waited. Eventually, Johnny tried but couldn't clasp his hand around the mug. He shoved it away and punched the table. "Jesus, Jules!"

Very tenderly, she reached out and placed her hand on his arm. "Hey."

He lowered his head.

JANUARY 18, 2017

Early Wednesday morning, they were back in the ER waiting to be seen by a doctor. This time, Jules was pacing, and Johnny was sitting on the gurney.

"We don't need to be here," said Johnny.

"Shush," said Jules.

"I'm saying we could make an appointment and see Dr. Davis next week. It's not an emergency."

"You didn't sleep last night because it hurt so much. As far as I'm concerned, it is an emergency," responded Jules. "I just hope we don't get little Hallie Jackson again."

As if on cue, Dr. Hallie Jackson walked in.

There were hellos and pleasantries, and she examined his arm for less than a minute.

"I want to get some pictures, but I can tell you now it's broken."

I knew it.

"Damn."

"I imagine it happened when you two 'fell' on the ice. Then, when you split the log, the impact exacerbated it."

The doctor's air quotes made it clear that she knew Johnny and Jules were full of shit. Johnny wasn't surprised.

"Well, what happens now?"

"As I said, we take some X-rays. Then, if it's as bad as I suspect, we put it in a cast, and hopefully, it heals."

"What kind of usage will he have while in a cast?" asked Jules.

Doctor Jackson looked annoyed by the question.

Give it a rest, Jules.

Johnny was annoyed by his wife's obsession with killing the President-elect and also wanted to get out of there as soon as possible.

"I have a big hunting trip next week," said Johnny, worried Jules might let her truth slip.

"No. You don't have a hunting trip coming up anymore," said Dr. Jackson.

Jules tried to say something, but the doctor cut her off. "Frankly, I suspect it's not a hunting trip but some other dumb event that you two are, for some reason, hiding from me. Just like the one that led to your injuries in the first place."

Jules said unconvincingly, "We fell on the ice."

"Sure. Okay. Look, at your age, bones don't heal with the same speed or guarantees as when you were younger. The damage you did to it will prevent you from doing the simplest things without immense pain. Your right hand is out of commission for a good six to eight weeks. Sorry."

Johnny could not believe his luck. Sure, his hand hurt like a son of a bitch, but he also just got a get-out-of-jail-free card. Jules would have to see that this was the end of her delusion. This was like guys who got shot in the ass during combat. It sucked, but it was also a ticket home and could save a life.

When the doctor left, Johnny got off the gurney, straightened his pants, and looked at his wife. What could he say?

"Come on, let's get the X-ray and cast, and then go to Rocco's for lunch."

CHAPTER 18

WALKING INTO THEIR HOUSE, JULES was livid.

Here we are again, home sweet fucking home. Let's go inside and keep busy doing nothing until it's time to eat again, put the goddamn TV on, and then go to bed. Get up tomorrow and do the same shit until we die. Great. Fine. Whatever.

When Johnny walked into the kitchen at dinner time, she almost lost it.

"I'm not making dinner tonight."

"Oh. Okay," said Johnny.

"I quit."

Johnny only said, "I'll order a pizza."

"I don't give a flying rat's ass," said Jules.

"Jules."

"What? Don't Jules me."

"You're acting as if this is my fault. I'm as disappointed as you," lied Johnny.

"Shut up. You're not disappointed. You're relieved. Your depressed wife's stupid plan is ruined, and you think that gets you off scot-free."

She waved her arms in the air in a shut-up gesture, and Johnny looked confused.

"Oh, go order your pizza and shove it in your stupid mouth."

And with that, Jules stormed out of the room.

JANUARY 19, 2017

The next day, things at the Coletti house reset. There was a silent breakfast, lunch at Rocco's, and a procedural book on tape in the Ford. Slowly, Jules could feel herself getting pulled into the murkiness. She decided to make a concerted effort to let go of being angry all the time and instead lean into being full-on depressed.

That night, Gina, Carl, and Becca came over. On the table was an old-school meatloaf with a stripe of tomato sauce down the middle—the way Carl liked it. She also made mashed potatoes, broccolini, and an oven-warmed loaf of Italian bread. Appetites were big. Tensions were high.

Gina was still half furious, half concerned about catching Jules joyriding with her daughter and made no effort to hide her frustration. Throughout the meal, Gina barely spoke. When she did, it was sarcastic or outright mean. Meanwhile, Jules did her best to keep things civil. "Do you hear anything from Charlie?"

Gina ignored her.

"He calls every single day," said Becca.

"Most kids go off to college, and their moms and dads have to beg them to call. Not Charlie. That kid calls us every day, without fail," said Carl as he helped himself to another piece of meatloaf.

"That's nice, though," said Johnny.

"It is. It is," said Carl, adding, "But sometimes this kid wants to talk, and I'm like, enough. I'm in the middle of *Iron Man* or something."

"No joke, you've seen that movie over twenty times," said Becca.

"Yeah. It's a great movie," said Carl.

"Anyway . . . Charlie needs a girlfriend," said Becca.

"Don't we all," joked Johnny.

Jules winced. "Good luck with that."

"I'll set you up with a Tinder account, Pappi," said Becca.

"I have no idea what that means, but thanks . . . ?" said Johnny.

"Oh, shush. And I think it's nice. It's proof of what good parents you two are. When Gina went to school, we only heard from her when she needed money," said Jules.

"Then, by your logic, that only proves what bad parents you and Dad were," said Gina.

Only Carl laughed.

Johnny looked at Jules, asking her to let it go with his eyes.

Suck it.

Jules turned to Becca, "And how are you doing being back at school?"

"Good. I have a chemistry project next week that will be fun."

"You're a weird bird, you know that?" said Johnny.

"I do!" Becca made weird bird noises and took a breath.

"What happened to the Pride Boys?" asked Jules.

"Proud Boys. And Daniel Braunger got suspended for having spray paint in his car," said Becca.

"Yeah, they said they couldn't prove that he painted the swastika. But having spray paint was bad enough to suspend him," said Carl.

"Bullshit technicality for not arresting him if you ask me," said a visibly pissed-off Gina.

"Oh, so you can say bullshit, but I can't even say crap?" asked Becca.

"Parent. Child. Get it?" said Gina.

Becca grimaced and said, "One good thing is that Mr. Adams said they might reinstitute the Debate Club but in a lesser capacity. Like, we'll have to do a fundraiser for any big trips out of state," said Becca.

"Does that mean you will get to go to the thing in Boston?" asked Jules.

"No. They said it's too late to raise enough cash for that this year. But next year, it should be okay."

"You'll be graduated by then," said Jules.

"That sucks. You led the damn revolution, and you don't get any of the rewards," said Johnny.

"Sure. But I'm happy those guys get it next year," said Becca.

There was a rare moment when no one had anything to say. Then Carl asked Johnny about his hand, and Johnny shrugged.

Carl ate more potatoes, Johnny ate more meatloaf, Becca devoured the broccolini, and Jules and Gina sulked silently.

After dinner, Carl and Johnny cleared the table, and, almost instinctively, Gina and Jules walked to the kitchen to do the dishes.

Jules watched as Gina went to the sink and started loading the dishwasher.

Jules' eyes went from Gina to the fridge, where she knew a lovely old bottle of Chardonnay was waiting to be drunk.

Haven't had a drink in almost two weeks, but what's the point? It is not like I need a clear head anymore.

Jules grabbed the white wine and poured a healthy glass.

There we go, delicious.

Mother and daughter stood in silence for a while, neither of them particularly interested in hearing what the other had to say. When Carl returned with a stack of plates, he loaded a few things in the dishwasher, dropped some dirtier ones into the sink, and told Gina that that was the last of it. Jules thanked him. He was rolling up his sleeves and about to pitch in with the pots and pans when Becca stuck her head in.

"Dad, you need to come downstairs. Pappi said that since his hand is hurt and he can't play me, he's going to teach you."

From the living room, Johnny yelled, "So someone besides me can kick her ass for once!"

"You wish," said Becca.

Gina patted Carl's back and said, "Go ahead. Mom and I will be down in a minute."

Jules got up and put both hands on Becca's shoulders. "Don't go easy on them. Play to win."

"You know it."

Carl and Becca left the kitchen.

Gina grabbed a dirty frying pan from the stove and started to scrub it.

"Leave those. I'll soak them, and your dad can wash them later," said Jules without looking up from the wine glass she was swirling.

Gina dried her hands, poured herself a glass of wine, and joined Jules at the table.

"Okay. But can we talk before we go downstairs?"

"Uh-oh. Here it comes."

"Don't be like that."

Jules said nothing.

"So, Carl and I are both worried about you and Dad," said Gina.

"Don't be. We're fine," said Jules.

"You're not fine."

"No, I guess we're not. But we're fine enough."

"Mom, this is serious. And Carl even agrees with me. I think . . . we think it's time to start talking about alternative living situations for you two."

"Not this again."

"Yes. This again."

"I get it. You're pissed at me. Fine. But please tell me you're not about to talk about putting us in a home again?"

"This isn't about being pissed at you. I'm worried about you and Dad. You're both acting weird, and, frankly, you both look like crap."

"Thanks."

"Sorry, but you do. You have scrapes all over you. And I heard you were in the ER last week?"

"Oh, that."

"Yeah, that! Why didn't you two say anything to me?"

"I never said anything because I didn't want you to worry."

"Well, you were right. Because I am."

"I can't believe Becca ratted us out," said Jules.

"Becca? How would she know?"

Now, Jules was confused.

"I ran into Barbara Jackson at Wawa, and she said her daughter had seen you and Dad there."

Goddamn, that little Hallie Jackson. Although I'm glad, Becca is still true blue.

"You should have told me. And now Dad's arm is in a cast. I mean, you guys are falling and hurting yourselves! It's scary."

"It's not scary. We slipped on the ice."

"So you say. But you can't attribute everything to accidents and senior moments. Riding around with my daughter in those nasty water pipes? What the heck is that?! You shouldn't be riding a motorcycle alone in a damn parking lot, let alone with a teenager in the sewers. It's dangerous and disgusting!"

"It wasn't a sewer."

"Mom."

"Well, no need to worry because that's all over now."

"What does that even mean?" asked Gina.

Jules lifted the glass to her mouth. After she downed the last of it, she raised it high, tapped the bottom with her hand, and got every last drop down her throat. Gina cringed.

For a few seconds, they just sat there. As far as Jules was concerned, the conversation was over.

Eventually, Gina spoke, "Okay. I was hoping we could talk about this. I was hoping that you would see the reality of your situation in a moment of clarity."

"Reality shmeality," said Jules.

"Fine, Mom. I didn't want to have to do it like this. But last night, Carl and I spoke with our lawyer. According to her, there's enough evidence to petition the county's adult protective services for guardianship and win."

"Guardianship of whom?" slurred a buzzed Jules.

"You and Dad. We've already talked to Doctor Jackson, and she's willing to cooperate," said Gina.

That shut Jules up.

After a long pause, Jules finally said, "You can't do that."

"We can, and we are. No matter what you think, you are not okay, Mom. You've been drinking an insane amount, not to mention acting recklessly," said Gina.

"You mean I've been happy? God forbid your old mother enjoy herself."

"No. I mean, you're acting crazy. And lying to me about it."

"How have I lied to you?" asked Jules.

"For one, Dad said he was working on the coffee table at Richie's last week, but I saw it in the living room earlier, and it needs refinishing as much as ever."

"I don't know anything about that."

"Also, you said you meant to text Becca the other day and texted me by mistake. I know that it wasn't a mistake. You wanted me to find you there. I just don't know why."

"Because no matter what you think of me, I was doing what was best for that kid."

"I believe you about that. And I know how much you love her and how much she loves you guys."

Jules smiled.

"So, what is it then? What's gotten into you two? If your thoughts are getting murky or cloudy, there are medications or treatments to help. If you guys are in a facility where people can watch you and ensure you're okay, we can get through this."

"Please."

"These places aren't the same as they used to be. You can still have autonomy and a kitchen, but there are also professionals on-site that can help and a community so you two can stay active," said Gina.

"Goddamnit. Everybody is constantly making assumptions about me. Assumptions, assumptions, assumptions, assumptions. I got your dad thinks I'm a little kid with a silly idea, my doctor believes my husband is abusing me, and now my daughter assumes I'm losing my marbles."

"Mom."

"Oh, shush."

Jules had been stuck for over fifty years because under her mountain of lethargy and sadness was a deep pool of rage. Having the man who had hurt Sheila permeate the news cycle for months had caused an intense heat of grief and trauma, the pressure of which was pushing the anger up. The fury was rising and forcing its way to the surface. Jules Coletti was about to erupt.

"It sounds crazy, but it's all over now, so you can relax. But for a brief moment, your dad and I were considering . . . thinking about . . ."

"What?!"

Jules took Gina's glass and swallowed her wine.

"Assassinating the President."

Gina raised her hands in a what-the-hell gesture.

"You know that I went to school with him?"

"Mom, I swear to God I have no idea what you are talking about. This is exactly—"

Jules cut Gina off by picking up the newspaper from Johnny's stack on the table. She pointed at a picture on the front cover."

"What?"

"Him. I was going to try to kill him."

Gina looked down at the paper and saw a picture of the President-elect."

"You were going to try and kill the next president of the United States?!"

Jules just shrugged.

"Okay, fine. Thanks for proving my point that you need to be institutionalized."

"Oh, shut up. You don't know him. He's a monster. A goddamn monster!"

"If you don't want to tell me what's going on, that's fine," said Gina.

Jules was becoming more buzzed but remained resolute.

"I am telling you. I knew that man at college. He's ignorant, evil, and soulless. And so yes, I wanted to—want to—kill him. For the greater good."

Another what-the-fuck look from Gina.

Finally, Gina said, "I have no idea what to do with that information."

Gina poured more wine and took a big sip as her mother stared at the table. Jules' mind was all over the place. She was thinking about all the opportunities her daughter and granddaughter had. She was thinking about her dumb dental assistant job and that she always felt underused working there. That job was how she identified herself, but it wasn't even full-time. That idiot Dr. Klein deliberately kept her at part-time so he wouldn't have to provide benefits.

Jules was also thinking about how she had somehow ended up with the life that Sheila had always wanted. She was the one who dreamed of being a housewife and a mother.

God forbid I say I never wanted to be a mom. Fucking blasphemy.

Even if Jules ever said such a thing, they would say she was hysterical; poor Jules had become melancholy.

Jules and Johnny were once at a dinner party playing some dumb game with other couples, and they had to draw a picture representing their spouses. Johnny had drawn a sad face, which irked Jules because she knew that that was the way everyone saw her.

I wasn't sad. I was pissed off. Oh well, more goddamn assumptions.

But she eventually forgave him for not seeing her the way she wanted to be seen. Jules was the one who had abandoned her dreams. She was the people pleaser. She was the one who, as her mother would say, "ate crumbs" so everyone else could have a full meal.

People like to talk about forgiveness, especially as they get older. Maybe that's a good thing. If you live long enough and are honest enough with yourself, even a little bit, and if you can get over your own nonsense, you can eventually forgive other people.

Gina finished the wine and, for once, didn't say anything. Jules had never seen her this quiet. *She hasn't told me that I'm doing something wrong in almost five full minutes. Must be a new record! She'll see. When I was her age, I thought I would never be able to forgive my parents. But then, you know, time and death happen.*

"My mother was cold. She wasn't necessarily mean; she just didn't show her emotions. She wasn't huggy. I wanted her to be huggier. I think I needed more hugs."

"Yeah. Grandma was weird."

"And Dad, well, he was who he was. But as I've gotten older, I've learned to forgive them. I understand that they did the best they could with the tools they had. And I can forgive friends and people who wronged me. Even your father."

Jules reached for Gina's hand, "And I hope you can forgive me. I know you wanted a brother or sister. Trust me, I grew up an only child and was jealous of all my friends who had siblings to keep them company. Your dad and I tried. He wanted more kids so much, but my body couldn't. I could get pregnant; that was never our problem, but I couldn't keep . . ."

Jules trailed off as she began to cry.

"Oh, Mom." Gina squeezed her mom's hand. "You don't need to apologize to me. I'm so sorry you had to go through that. That must have been so hard."

Jules sat up, wiped her eyes, and shook it off.

"Oh well. What are you going to do? Life is life. My point is that there are some people we can forgive and others are unforgivable. Some actions you don't get closure on. And those people don't deserve absolution. What he did to Sheila, he didn't push those pills down her throat, but he might as well have. He killed her. And that killed me. I didn't have the courage; I mean, I tried. I tried to tell people. But I gave up."

Jules told Gina about how the term "date rape" didn't exist in 1968, even though there was a long history of men forcing women they knew to have sex with them. She told her daughter that she and Sheila had gone to the school's dean to report him, and the dean had told them that they were overreacting. The older man said that he was an outstanding student from an outstanding family and that maybe he had misunderstood Sheila's intentions, and perhaps she had mis-understood what she was signaling. Gina gasped when Jules told her that the dean had told Sheila that if she wanted him to go forward with an investigation, she would risk being expelled for engaging in illicit sexual activity on campus.

There were lots of hugs and tears between Gina and Jules.

Eventually, Jules stood up, straightened her clothes, wiped her eyes with the backs of her hands, and said, "Anyway, my plan for revenge, which never really included your daughter in any way, is all over now. File it under another thing I almost did that will not happen."

"Mom. I am so sorry for everything you just told me. I can't even imagine the pain you must feel. But talking about assassinating the president only confirms my fears about your and Dad's mental acuity."

And we're back.

"Please, forget I even said anything. It's all over now. I promise. A momentary lapse of reason. You go downstairs and watch your husband get his butt handed to him by my granddaughter at table tennis."

And with that, Jules got up and made her way to the sink, "I'll soak these pans and be right down."

Gina looked as if she wanted to say more or to do something, but Jules did her best to non-verbally communicate that she needed to be alone. It worked because, without saying another word, Gina hugged her mom and went downstairs.

CHAPTER 19

JANUARY 20, 2017

JOHNNY SPENT MOST OF THE morning doing nothing in the basement, avoiding Jules. But it was freezing outside, and he couldn't hide from his wife all day. About an hour before noon, he decided getting Jules out of the house would be a good idea. He knew the news would be wall-to-wall coverage of the inauguration, and Jules was crazed enough without being forced to see him sworn in as the president of the United States.

Johnny was self-aware enough to know he was a stoic man and that emoting wasn't easy for him. Maybe it was his upbringing, the war, or just his wiring. Either way, Johnny knew Richie would be better for Jules that day.

When they arrived, Richie put some logs in the fireplace and made hot chocolate. They sat around the small kitchen table, sipping their cocoa and looking out at the barn. Richie mentioned that it felt like they would get more snow. Johnny agreed, and Jules said nothing.

After a bit, Richie offered Johnny a cigar, and the two men lit up.

"You okay, Jules?" asked Richie.

Leave it alone, would ya?

"Yeah," she answered.

"It's a shitty day all around," said Richie.

"Yeah," said Jules, who turned and scowled at her husband.

"It's not even the inauguration that's got her all pissy. She's still mad that we won't make the history books," said Johnny, slightly condescendingly.

Richie nodded. "Well, at least you guys tried."

Some more cigar puffs.

"Did we, though?" asked Jules.

Johnny sat up. "Of course we did."

"But as soon as we hit a bump, we folded."

Johnny held up his cast and pointed at it with his good hand. "I can't shoot. What do you want from me?"

"I know all about it."

Silence.

"What if you taught me?" asked Jules.

Johnny laughed. Jules did not. Richie kept quiet.

Finally, Johnny stood up. He was legitimately mad. "Wait. Are you being serious? Jesus. It took me months of training and years in-country to do what I do. You expect me to show you in two weeks? Come on. That's insulting."

"You trained to set up the shot, adjust for external forces and angles, and all that crap. You can use your training to do all that again. All I have to do is pull the trigger," said Jules.

"She has a point. You could do all the prep," interjected Richie.

Johnny looked at his friend. "Oh. So now the draft dodger is an expert too?" He turned back to Jules. "Do you have any idea what it takes to kill someone? I'm not talking about pointing and squeezing. Keeping steady while doing that isn't as easy as you make it out to be, and God willing, you don't miss and accidentally kill an innocent person. But imagine getting up each day knowing you killed someone's father or husband, not to mention the fact that this whole thing has been insane from the start. We almost died practicing the escape. The truth is, we'd probably end up in jail or worse before we even left that hotel. It was a dumb fucking idea from the get-go."

"Screw you," said Jules.

"Yeah. Screw me. And screw you too," said Johnny.

"I mean, if we're all getting screwed, then go ahead and screw me too," said Richie. Johnny appreciated his friend's attempt to add levity to the tense situation but knew it was pointless.

Jules got up and walked outside. Richie started to get up to go after her, but Johnny stopped him.

"Let her go. We'll all be better off after she cools down a bit."

"I guess."

Richie sat back down. "But you were pretty harsh with her if you ask me."

"Luckily, I didn't."

"Blow me."

Johnny smiled. The two sat in silence, puffing on the cigars.

JULY 1950

Johnny was five years old when his dad got a job at the Lukens Steel Company, a few towns over from Warrensburg, Pennsylvania, and announced to his family that they would be leaving the Bronx. During the next three weeks, Johnny had to say goodbye to all his friends and help his folks load the rented truck parked outside their brownstone's stoop. As they drove off, he stared out the window at the corner bodega and already missed the sound his upstairs neighbors made walking above his bedroom ceiling. Moving from that urban comfort to the chaotic boredom of the suburbs bummed young Johnny Colletti out.

Once they arrived, Johnny played on their new front lawn with sticks and dirt as his dad and a friend unloaded the truck. Johnny stayed out of their way because he knew his dad was pissed off about having to leave New York and had already downed a few beers on the drive. He had also referred to their new home as being in the "God-forsaken sticks" about a hundred times. To make matters worse, Johnny's mom wouldn't be joining them until the following day, as she was spending the night with a family friend in the Bronx with Johnny's one-and-a-half-year-old brother.

When Johnny saw a skinny kid walk up the dirt driveway, he immediately stood up, expecting that the kid wanted to fight. Instead, Richie walked over, reached into his pocket, and pulled out a frog. Being from a city, Johnny had never seen a frog, and he was in awe.

"Can I hold it?"

Richie handed the amphibian to little Johnny.

"You can keep it," said Richie.

And that was that—best friends for life.

JANUARY 20, 2017

As the two old friends enjoyed their cigars, Johnny couldn't help but feel good. He wasn't sure where Jules was, but it didn't matter much. She would get over it eventually, and things would return to normal. But the creak of the barn doors as Jules opened them disturbed the peace and quiet.

First, Richie, then Johnny, jumped up and went outside. They saw Jules walk out of the barn and to the pickup, where she retrieved Johnny's rifle case from behind the driver's seat.

Oh, Jesus fucking Christ on a friggin' popsicle stick. Jules! Put that down before someone gets seriously hurt.

"JULES!"

She ignored him and marched across the lawn to the tree with the ladder. She strapped the rifle case around her neck when she got there and started climbing.

"Is she going to injure herself? What's the recoil like on that thing?" said Richie.

"Don't act like you know anything about shooting, you hippie."

Richie laughed.

"It's a bolt-action rifle, which means it's not so bad," said Johnny.

They continued to smoke and watch as Jules scaled the tree.

"Although the fact that she can even lug that thing up the tree is something."

"For your information. I'm honored to be called a hippie." Richie flashed the peace sign and sang, "Hey, hey, LBJ, how many kids did you kill today?"

Johnny smiled, "In retrospect, you may have been on the right side of that one."

"I guess. But I always admired you for going," said Richie.

"Yeah."

"Seriously. And please forgive me if this sounds too fluffy for your taste, but I was proud of you. Even a little jealous of your sense of duty."

There were a few more long, stoic puffs from their cigars as they watched Jules make her way to the deer stand.

"She seems determined," said Richie.

"As always."

Johnny watched as she assembled, loaded, and set up the rifle on a stand. Once the clicking of the assembly stopped, it was eerily silent. Then she took the shot.

The bullet entered the side of Johnny's pickup truck.

Johnny handed his cigar to Richie and sprinted to the tree. Jules saw him and yelled down, "Well, you going to help me aim this thing or what?"

"Are you kidding? No! I am not helping you! You shot my truck."

"Goddamnit. That's my point. I need your help. And it's OUR truck, you asshole."

"Oh, man. This is my fault. I should have stopped this from the get-go. I knew that somehow your perverted, warped brain really believed that we would do this. But we never were. I never had any intention of going through with any of this. You're cracking up. Seriously, we talk about it all the time with our friends. How do you know? How do you know when you're starting to lose your mind? Well, this is it. We know! You've gone cuckoo."

"If you never intended to do it, why were you humoring me?"

"Exactly that. I was humoring you. I was enjoying who you were with this crazy idea in your head. It's like you started to like me again. You've hated me for so long that I had given up on it. Why rock the boat? But then, the past few weeks, Jesus Christ, I don't know. It was fun!"

"Give me a break."

"No. You asked. I knew if I told you the truth, you would get sad, and we'd be back where we are right now."

"Mad! Not sad. And I have liked the past couple of weeks too. The way you acted with Jordan was so funny. That little twirp. And it was fun, the night in the hotel."

Johnny's eyes softened. He wanted to reach her. "Yeah. It was a good night, Jules. We can have more of those nights, but this has to stop now."

She flipped him off, readjusted the gun, and got ready to take another shot.

Johnny walked back over to Richie, picked up his hot chocolate, and said, "We should head in before the next one hits us."

From the tree stand, Jules yelled, "Chicken shit!"

CHAPTER 20

AFTER DINNER, JOHNNY WENT TO the Acorn Pub with the guys, and Jules found herself on the couch, flipping through the channels. She landed on some boring British crime show tailored for women her age. Jules poured herself a glass of wine, opened a box of Double-Stuffed Oreos, and was about to numb the day away when she saw her reflection on the TV screen. Gina was right. She looked like shit.

Screw this. I'm too mad to be depressed right now.

Jules poured the wine down the drain and went upstairs to find that sunflower dress she had bought at Nordstrom Rack a few years ago but never had the occasion or confidence to wear. She dressed, put on some makeup, and even sprayed her neck with good old Chanel No. 5. She rushed into the garage, fired up the Triumph, and was off.

Her first stop was the Figaro Bakery. When she arrived at 6:55 pm, they had just locked the door. But when the normally acerbic clerk saw the troubled older woman outside wearing a vintage motorcycle jacket over a yellow and green dress, he took pity on her and let her in. Jules over thanked the clerk and snatched up the last two chocolate croissants. From the pâtisserie, she headed over to Soup House. She had planned to sit in a booth and eat that goddamn lobster bisque all by herself and finish it off with the pastry. But when the pimply-faced boy asked if she wanted her soup here or to go, Jules unexpectedly said to go.

Outside, she put the oversized bag in the Triumph's luggage box, popped up the kickstand, and peeled out of the gravel parking lot.

She knew where Tim Decker lived because he had moved back into his parents' house when they died in '98. Jules and Tim had a pleasant conversation outside Wegman's supermarket soon after his return. He was so happy to see her that he blushed when she said hello. Jules knew that didn't necessarily mean he didn't have a girlfriend, but she figured that if she didn't go to his house to see him right then, she never would.

What do I have to lose?

Jules pulled up to the small white and red house and was glad to see there were no streetlights on Tim's block. She parked, removed her helmet, got her soup, and stood behind an old Maple tree, trying to decide what to do next. Thirty minutes later, Jules had eaten half of the soup, which was too buttery for her taste, when she saw the man she was there to have an affair with through the front window. Tim was sitting on a couch in the living room, reading a book. He was attractive, had all his hair, and, for an old guy, was fit. Unlike Jules or Johnny, it seemed Tim took care of himself. He had good posture and modern clothes, and a dog was chewing on a toy at his feet. It could not look more idyllic. Jules smiled but quickly stopped when a woman in her early forties came into the room and sat beside him on the couch.

Didn't realize he had a daughter.

Jules was intrigued as she reflexively ate another spoonful of bisque.

Inside the house, Tim got up and put a record on the turntable, and then he and the lady started to dance.

Oh, come on.

They danced for a while and then kissed, and not like a father and daughter would kiss.

Are you kidding me? She's a goddamn child.

Tim and his lady friend walked to the back of the house, and the dog followed.

Oh. I bet they both shit rainbows.

She went to the front of the house, hurled her soup all over the door, and laughed. She stepped back, picked up the container, and used her spoon to scrape one last spoonful and put it into her mouth as she smirked at the mess she had made.

She retrieved the two croissants from the luggage rack and was about to take a delicious bite when a car turned the corner and its headlights shone on her. Jules dove to the ground and crawled behind a tree, scared of being seen. It was not her best moment. When she stood up, she noticed she had landed on and ruined her much-anticipated sweet treat.

I need help.

Jules slunk back to the Triumph and got on.

After she put the bike back in the garage, she noticed that the woodpile was still a mess from when Johnny had abandoned it after hurting his hand. When she picked up the axe to put in the shed, it felt good in her hands. She still had her riding gloves on, so she figured, why not? Chopping wood will feel good. She felt invigorated when she lifted the axe and split the first log. Her heart was racing, and she could feel the physical activity exorcising the demons from her mind. Just like that, all her aches from the first slide down the laundry chute disappeared.

But twenty minutes later, they all came back.

Shit. What the hell am I doing out here?

Jules dropped the axe and sat on the ground. She was so frustrated and mad that the cold didn't affect her as she thought about her attempt to—for the first time in her life—have an affair. The silliness of the idea shattered Jules' shame of failing, and she laughed at herself.

What an idiot.

She didn't even want to sleep with Tim Decker. She just wanted a well-deserved vacation from her reality. All her married friends from church had similar relationships to hers and Johnny's. One person would watch TV upstairs while their spouse watched TV downstairs. One person would go out with friends to a bar, a movie, or a book club while the other stayed home and read. They would eat together over a thousand times a year with fewer than a hundred words spoken between them. Everyone she knew who had been married for over thirty years was in a business arrangement and going through the motions on a treadmill of mediocrity.

Long-term loveless marriages were not just accepted by her peers but expected. Cohabitating with someone you didn't like was okay. Jules and Johnny split the work. She did the cooking and cleaning, and Johnny kept up the car and the house and did the shopping. They had each other if something bad happened, to give a ride to a doctor, or to sit across from at a restaurant to avoid feeling sad when the waiter takes away the extra place setting, leaving the individual alone staring at the wall. Surely, tolerating Johnny had been better than leaving him. The kind of extraordinary change that being single would have brought was impossible to imagine. She never tried to talk to Johnny about her wants because she knew that change was hard. Jules knew that she and Johnny were locked in.

That's when it hit her: with or without Johnny, she was locked in. Jules was stuck in that dorm hallway in 1968 after hearing the news that her best friend had killed herself. Sure, her body had gotten old. She had wrinkles, gray hair, and bad knees, but emotionally, Jules was nineteen. The realization gave Jules the chills.

Now what?

One hour later, Jules decided to unarrest her development, to rip herself out of the amber of trauma. For the first time since she first spoke aloud about assassination at Rocco's, Jules realized that she had never truly believed they would kill him. She had been so focused on her anger at Johnny for not taking it seriously that her rage became the fuel that moved her forward, despite never taking it seriously herself. But right then and there, sitting on the snow, an axe in front of her and a full moon above her, Jules knew she had to do it—not because she needed to make her own decisions, or even for Sheila, revenge, or justice, but so that she could move on with her life. Knowing that, nothing could stop her, not Johnny's arm in a cast, her inability to shoot a gun, her daughter's threat to lock her up, a drunk-ass retired cop turned security guard, or the lack of a viable escape plan. None of the obstacles in Jules' path mattered anymore. She was one hundred percent committed.

She went to Johnny's truck to look for his rifle. She would teach herself how to shoot the damn thing or die trying. The hell with Johnny's negativity. She could figure it out herself, but the rifle was not in the pickup. She went inside and searched the entire house. Jules searched in their bedroom closet, under the bed, and above the hutch. It was nowhere.

Son of a bitch!

CHAPTER 21

AT THE ACORN PUB, ED, Richie, and Johnny were at the bar sipping their beers and nursing their shots of whiskey. Johnny appreciated that, besides the ambient noise, the place was silent.

"Thanks," said Ed as the bartender dropped a plate of nachos in front of him. Ed reached for a giant chip loaded with melted cheese and pulled pork and shoved it into his mouth. Richie grimaced as Ed devoured the loaded nachos.

With his mouth still full, Ed said to Richie, "You want me to order you a cheese plate?"

Johnny grabbed a chip. "Give it a rest, Ed, would ya."

Richie waved him off. "No. It never gets old. I've been a vegan for over fifteen years now, and he makes the same crack every time I see him. Hilarious."

"I was trying to be empathetic," said Ed, full of chips and sarcasm.

"Well, if you knew anything about anything, you'd know that vegans don't eat cheese."

"Must have missed that issue of Newsweek," said Ed.

Richie downed his shot. "You, sir, are a rube."

"I am. But at least I am a consistent rube," said Ed.

"The way you two argue, you'd think you were married," said Johnny.

"Whatever. I just don't get how a guy who has owned a working farm for five decades decides to be a vegan. What, did you fall in love with a cow?" said Ed.

"I think you have mistaken him for Linda," joked Johnny.

Richie and Johnny laughed. Ed didn't.

"To tell you the truth, I did fall in love with a sheep named Mary once. She was funny and smart and so, so kind. But the best thing about Mary, besides the beautiful wool she gave me every season, was that she was the best kisser I have ever had the pleasure of kissing," said Richie.

Then they all laughed.

"I find deer attractive. I'd kiss a doe," said Ed in a way-too-serious tone.

They all laughed again and took sips of their beers.

Just then, Jules burst in.

"Jonathan Vincent Coletti!"

"Oh, crap. What have I done now?" said Johnny.

"You know goddamn well what you did."

"I swear to God I do not."

She folded her arms and stared at him.

"I honestly have no idea what is happening right now."

"Where is your rifle?" asked Jules.

"The key word being 'my,' as in, *my* rifle."

"Oh, knock it off. You hid it so I couldn't practice anymore. You hid it from me!"

"Yes. I did. Because you have got to get this dumb idea out of your head."

Realizing they were talking about this in front of Ed, Johnny turned to him and bullshitted, "She wants me to take her hunting."

He turned back to Jules, "And that's an insane idea."

"Why do you get to decide we're done? Why do you ALWAYS DECIDE EVERYTHING? THIS TIME I DECIDE! I GET TO DECIDE!"

Johnny went to say something, but Jules uttered a loud, primal scream that silenced him and the entire bar. She grabbed Richie's shot and poured it in his lap, she slammed the shot glass on the floor, and walked out.

Johnny watched his wife leave and felt more guilty than mad but did nothing.

"Finally, some excitement around this morgue," said Ed, who turned to the bartender, "Quincy, three more shots. I'm buying."

Johnny was shocked. "You're buying?"

"What can I say? It warms my heart to see a lady take an interest in shooting an animal."

Richie mimed writing on a piece of paper. "Okay. Sexism . . . check. Congrats, Ed. It's not even nine yet, and you've checked all the ignorance boxes. Good job."

"Blow me."

Richie and Johnny laughed at how mad Ed got when Richie gave him shit.

After the excitement wound down and the bartender gave them their shots, Richie suddenly grabbed his side. It looked like it hurt him like hell as he got up.

"You okay?" said Johnny.

"Yeah. I just need—"

Dread filled Johnny's soul as he watched his best friend fall to the ground.

CHAPTER 22

JULES WAS DEEPLY ASLEEP WHEN her phone alarm woke her up.

What?

Shit. It wasn't a dream. Oh, Richie.

"Jesus, could that thing be any louder?" said Johnny.

A bad start to a bad day.

Jules slid out of bed and walked to the bathroom. She wanted to sleep the week away but knew she had to keep moving. The day was going to be hard enough without starting late.

An hour later, Jules was at the kitchen table in a black dress, eating a piece of peanut butter toast. And Johnny, in a black suit, was at the stove. He scooped some oatmeal into a bowl, shook cinnamon over it, and sat next to Jules. There was no conversation or eye contact.

The quiet was disturbed when the teapot whistled. Jules used the hot water to make French press coffee, then crossed to the fridge, took some half-and-half, and sat back at the table.

After breakfast, they backed the truck out of the driveway and drove in silence for a good while.

Finally, Jules spoke. "Linda said last night that Kay flew in."

"That's nice."

"I mean, she and Richie were married for twenty-two years."

"Yeah, but it's been even longer since they split, and what with only three days' notice."

"True. To put the man in the ground only three days after dying seems awfully quick," said Jules.

"That's what he wanted. I think he figured if it were a rush job, fewer people would make a fuss," said Johnny.

"Yeah."

More silence.

"Well, if we get divorced, you don't have to come to my funeral," said Johnny.

Funny.

Johnny went to start his audiobook but stopped.

Poor Johnny. He was hurting so much but would never admit it, not even to his wife. She knew enough to wait for him to talk about it, so she let her mind drift and thought about how much she loved Richie. He was her best friend, too. He was also her ally when Johnny, Gina, and Carl would team up against her. He was warm and kind and never scared to show Johnny and Jules how much he loved them.

Pull it together. It's going to be a long day.

Out of nowhere, Johnny said, "I know you're still pissed. But honestly, I never thought we were going to do it. I'm sorry for confusing you. I should have just said no from the start."

"Confusing me? Shush. You have no idea. To you, it was having fun; that's what you said, right? Well, it was more than that to me. It was important."

"And having fun is important to me. I don't know when it became a thing that only young people can have fun, but I hate that crap. Planning this all out, riding the bike again, and even shooting those cutouts in Richie's barn was exciting, and we were doing it together. Like we were kids or something. And I know you felt that because we were making eye contact. Maybe that sounds idiotic, but you haven't looked at me in years."

"I look at you."

"No, you don't. No one does. Since I retired from Goodyear, I've become invisible. People used to be happy to see me or, I guess, annoyed by me, but now they don't even notice I'm there. It's like I get up, think about what I'm going to eat, do some chores, and then go back to bed. I'm like a dog under the table. You know it's always there, but you don't see it."

"That's not true."

Oh my God. He is hurting so much. Why doesn't he say what is really troubling him? The last of his family is gone, and he feels alone. Jules knew what that felt like.

"Yes, it is. If I died, who would be worse off?"

Jules said nothing.

"That's what I thought. I'm sure you've fantasized about what your life would be like without me."

All the time.

"No, I have not."

"Liar. It's natural. Truth be told, we'd both be happier if I were dead."

Jules laughed as they pulled into a parking spot at their church. Johnny caught his pant leg on the bumper outside the car and got a small rip on his knee.

"Oh, for the love of."

Jules brushed the dirt off the ripped area. "It's fine."

"In the scheme of things, yeah."

They walked for a bit in silence. Seeing the other people, some in couples, some walking alone toward the church, Jules appreciated having Johnny with her. She had often wondered if Richie was lonely in that big old house. Jules and Johnny had invited Richie to every holiday and family dinner. Still, he was alone in the dark all those other nights, dealing with all the shit life throws at you as your body starts to fall apart, your mind turns to mush, and society dismisses you as an irrelevant placeholder. Having Johnny in her life kept Jules alert and connected. Maybe that's not "love" as others define it, but if helping one exist isn't love, what the hell is?

Poor Richie.

Johnny stopped to let other mourners walk past. "I know I don't always say things right—"

"You think?" interrupted Jules.

"More than you imagine."

A shared smile.

"What I was trying to say about having fun was that the past few days have felt different. Like that time we ate at Manny's when Gina was a baby, and we ditched without paying. Remember that? Just stupid fun. Seeing you happy and that glow in your eyes has been like old times."

"I agree. I've missed how much you used to make me laugh. And I get what you're saying about being seen. I miss seeing you look at me the way you have since that day at the hotel. And by the way, I went back and paid for our meal at Manny's. It wasn't right, stiffing the waitress like that."

He laughed.

She reached out, took his hand, and led him into the church.

A truce.

"Can't believe his service is in a church that he hasn't stepped inside in nearly forty years," said Johnny.

The Colettis were moving through the crowd, greeting and shaking hands with old friends, when Jules got a text.

"It's Gina. They're running late. They'll meet us at the cemetery."

"A little disrespectful if you ask me," said Johnny.

Jules knew better. She knew that Gina had important things to do, and being a few minutes late to a service was anything but disrespectful. Jules also knew that if Richie had been alive, he would have wanted Gina to be doing "other" things, but she thought it best not to share all that with Johnny just yet.

Johnny and Jules greeted more friends. Kay, Ed, and Linda went to their seats in the middle pew. Johnny took Jules' hand and said, "You know we can't do this. You do know that, don't you?"

"No. I don't."

Sighs all around.

Jules pulled her hand away from his and said, "And I'm sorry that retirement makes you feel useless and invisible. I am, but on the other hand, join the fucking club. I have felt that way ever since we got married. Ever since anyone stopped asking me what I thought about anything."

"That's not true."

"It is true. Because if you had bothered once to goddamn ask me, you would know that I hate Rocco's. You would know I've always wanted a dog and would rather jump in the ocean than sail around on a cruise ship."

"Okay, you're right. You don't like the same sandwich shop I do, so I should help you commit a federal offense. Sounds fair."

"No. You have no idea. I asked you to help me because my entire life has been paused, and I was hoping you could help me unpause it. That man has done—"

Their argument was interrupted when Father Kuppler walked to the altar.

"Hello, and welcome on this sad occasion as we prepare to bid farewell to Richie Devlin..."

There were lots of platitudes, some genuine sentiments, loads of structured grief, and another long story about food. An hour later, Johnny and Jules were driving in the funeral procession to the cemetery.

"I thought that was a nice service," said Jules.

"Yeah."

"And it was nice to see Kay."

"Her face looked weird."

"I think she's had some surgeries."

"Figures. Living in California makes everyone a nut." Johnny continued, "I can't believe that he's gone... He never said anything to you?"

"Not a word," lied Jules.

"The man has stage-four pancreatic cancer and carries on as if nothing's wrong. A stubborn mule to the end."

CHAPTER 23

JOHNNY PARKED AT THE CEMETERY, walked up the path to the gravesite, and joined a small group of mourners. Everyone was discussing what a lovely service it was, but Johnny wasn't listening. He was thinking about how weird it was that Richie was gone. He was thinking about how empty he felt inside. Johnny was no stranger to loss or death. No one who fought in a war or made it to his age could be. Even when he lost his folks, as dramatic as it was, Johnny didn't feel knocked off his axis from their absence. He had often heard people say they felt alone and without their moral compasses after their parents died, but that wasn't Johnny's experience. He felt nothing but relief when his parents died. When his dad's heart gave out back in '78, Johnny felt relieved that the monster could no longer hurt him. And when his mom died of cancer in '98, Johnny felt relieved that she was no longer in pain.

But suddenly, at the age of seventy-one, for the first time since he was five, he was devoid of his foundation.

Johnny spotted Gina and Carl and made his way over to them. Their disrespect pissed him off.

"Nice of you guys to show up."

"Sorry, Dad, it was a rough morning," said Gina.

Gina looked to Jules for help with Johnny, but Jules seemed to be thinking about something else.

After a few beats, Jules said, "Can you give your father and me a minute?" and she pulled Johnny off to the side.

"I can't keep going around and around with you on this, Jules," said Johnny.

"Fine. This is the last thing I'll say. Do you know how we always listen to your books and watch those crime shows you like on Netflix?"

"If this is about not choosing things, trust me, I'd be happy if you made more decisions. For the love of fucking God, we can watch whatever you want tonight if we can just let it go!"

Jules stepped back and folded her arms. "You done?"

Nothing.

"It's not about that. I'm trying to say that whenever I hear about something terrible happening to someone, like in those books, or a movie, or on the news, do you know what I do? I always wonder what you would do. What would Johnny do if someone tried to mug us? What would Johnny do if someone tried to hurt the grandkids?"

"I wouldn't let them," said Johnny.

"I know that. And I love you for it. But I recently realized that I never think about what I would do." She stopped and waited until a few people walked by. When they were alone again, she leaned in close to him. "I'm not even included in my own thoughts anymore."

"Jules."

"Do you know why I quit school? Why I left college?"

"Because of Sheila. I know." He tried to comfort her, but she pulled away.

"Kind of. That's what I say. But I had every intention of going back after her funeral. It was because of him. There was already talk around school that he had forced himself on other girls. And I was convinced, I knew—I was certain that if I went back, he would hurt me. It wasn't grief that derailed my plans. It was fear. And that asshole was the author of that fear."

NOVEMBER 8, 1968

It was the morning of Sheila's funeral, and Johnny, who was in his navy dress whites, sat on Jules' childhood bed upstairs in her parents' house, where Jules had been staying since leaving school.

Jules came out of the bathroom, wiped her sweaty brow, and stood in front of Johnny.

"You okay?"

"Yeah. I think I'm pregnant."

What? Johnny was stunned. His draw dropped, and his eyes focused on an Elvis poster on the far wall.

Money, apartments, Jule's parents, mine, I'll mess it up, diapers, clothes, a crib, the war, responsibility, squishy, hope, a new start . . .

"Are you going to say something?" asked Jules.

"Um. Are you sure?" asked Johnny.

"Pretty sure. I mean, I've never been pregnant before, but it sure feels like I always imagined it would feel. Plus, I'm sick and missed my period."

"Wow."

"Yeah."

"Do you think we should get married?"

"Aren't you the romantic?"

"Come on, Jules. We should get married."

Did she not want to marry him?

Jules pushed Johnny off the bed, forced him onto his knees, said yes, pulled him back up, shook his hand, and kissed him on the lips. He grabbed her waist, and the two started dancing to music that only they could hear. They danced for a long time, truly two people in love. It ended when Jules' mother yelled from downstairs for them to hurry. They looked at each other, no words necessary, and headed down.

It was a three-hour drive to Bernardsville, New Jersey, where Sheila's funeral was held. Jules' mom drove, Johnny rode shotgun, and Jules sat in the back. There was no music or conversation.

What Johnny didn't want to say to Jules was that he would most likely be going off to Vietnam soon. He was excited about being a dad, but the timing couldn't be worse.

The service was long, sad, and packed.

Afterward, at the Newmans' enormous house, as Johnny devoured a salami and cheese sandwich, he put his hand on Jules' stomach and said, "If you're only two months in, you should be able to finish this semester and still graduate on time."

"I'm not going back."

"What?"

"I'm not going back to school."

"What are you talking about? You love it."

"I don't want that anymore."

"You only have four more classes."

"I don't care."

"What about your dream? What about having a big office on Wall Street? Changing the world?"

"The hell with the goddamn world," said Jules.

"Come on. I know it will be a pain, but we can figure it out with the baby. If we got married, I'd get better housing and could watch the baby when I'm not on duty. And I'll bet one of our moms could help and keep the baby during the week."

Jules got quiet.

"I know it's been hard with losing Sheila and all. But she would want you to go back."

"No, she wouldn't."

"Of course, she would. Other than me, she was your biggest fan."

"Stop saying that! You have no idea what she would want!"

When Johnny went to hug Jules, she pushed him back. Jules had been so loud and forceful with Johnny that everyone turned to look at them. The uproar had caused a crying domino effect, starting with Sheila's dad, then her mother, cousins, and friends. Soon, everyone was in tears.

Jules used the wave of grief as cover to run. As she fled out the front door, Johnny froze. He was conflicted. Should he go after her even though she had just pushed him away, or stay put and give her space?

For the next hour, Johnny sat on the couch in the corner of the living room and lamented for Sheila, her parents, Jules, and even himself. The future was as uncertain as it had ever been, and he couldn't afford to do anything but trudge on. He had woken up that day thinking he needed to be there for Jules, and with the news of her pregnancy, that had only become more true—no time for self-pity.

He went to look for her outside and found her in her parents' yellow and brown, faux-paneled Ford station wagon. She was sobbing in the back seat when Johnny opened the front door and got in. He didn't look back or say a word. He sat in silence, facing forward. *Give her space.*

When he felt her hand on his shoulder, he said, "Okay. You ready to go back inside now?"

Jules wiped her tears away. "Yes."

They got out of the wagon and went back to the gathering.

JANUARY 24, 2017

Johnny looked at his wife standing before his best friend's grave. She was perfectly composed. Her face was stoic, and not a single part of her being was shaking, quivering, or uncertain of itself. She was wearing all black, and Johnny couldn't help but notice that Jules looked the same as she did all those years ago at *her* best friend's funeral. In his eyes, she was as beautiful as she was back then. But after hearing her words, he knew she was stuck in the same place she was that day, and it was time for her to move on.

He felt foolish for never realizing that Jules never returned to school out of fear. He had assumed she was depressed and sad, but she was scared of that godawful son of a bitch.

Johnny had always known that Jules' identity was shrouded in grief and fear and that something needed to be done, but if he was honest with himself, he didn't know what to do. That was the problem. For too long, both he and Jules thought that feeling of dread was there for good, and neither tried to do anything about it.

"I love you," said Johnny.

"I love you, too," said Jules.

It wasn't obligatory, and it wasn't insincere. At that moment, their love was alive for the first time in decades.

Johnny put his hands on the wooden box and took a deep breath. A single tear ran down his face, and Jules wiped it away.

CHAPTER 24

AT THE CRACK OF DAWN, Jules was lamenting. Sitting in the kitchen, her attention was focused on the painting that hung above the doorframe. It was one of Richie's last non-abstracts—an oil representation of his barn that he had made for Jules' fiftieth birthday. The way the natural light shone down on the snow-dusted roof always brought a smile to Jules' face, especially the way the dripping icicles gave a feeling of a changing season. It was as though despair was melting away to make room for new life and hope. The fondness Richie had felt for both the subject and the recipient of the painting was undeniable.

On that day, however, the painting made Jules' heart feel heavy. She was remembering how friends would talk about Richie's "perpetual singleness." Staying single after his divorce from Kay drew a lot of speculation about his sexual preferences—the usual small-town hearsay and rumors. To be honest, Jules had wondered dozens of times if Richie was gay. It made sense to her that if he were, he would keep it quiet, given the closed-mindedness of their community of older friends. Jules had considered bringing it up to Richie to let him know that she didn't give a rat's ass who he loved and that any person he cared about was always welcome in her home. In the end, she never broached the subject, if for no other reason than it wasn't her right, and she wanted to respect his privacy. Now that he was gone, Jules regretted never asking and giving him a space to talk about it. She wanted to believe that no matter what his personal life was or wasn't, he never felt anything other than love and support from her and Johnny. Jules mostly hoped that he had never felt lonely. He didn't appear to be, as far as she could tell; he was the most fulfilled person she knew.

Ruminating on Richie's happiness caused Jules to ponder her own. She had often felt a heaviness that she never thought would leave. She had always attributed it to Sheila's death and the missed opportunities caused by abandoning her dream of getting a business degree. Such trauma, grief, and disappointment at a young age molded the woman she became. When she was in her twenties and thirties, it would feel like a punch in the face. She'd be doing the laundry or playing with Gina at a playground, and out of nowhere, she would get hit with bouts of crippling hopelessness. But by the time she was fifty, it became less focused. It became a part of her, like a hand coming from behind and pushing her down. The sorrow became her skin. It just was, just like the way her eyes were blue and her hair was gray. Her essence was melancholy.

But suddenly, on that cold January morning, it struck Jules that much of that feeling had dissipated. It made no sense since nothing had changed. Sheila was still dead, and Jules had still never realized her dream of being a successful businesswoman. Yet, Jules felt like the murky, gray feeling in her belly had lessened.

What the hell? One of the people I loved most in this world was put in the ground yesterday, and now *I feel happy.*

As Jules got dressed, she became aware that the weight that had been lifted had nothing to do with Richie or Sheila. The newfound peace she felt came from the simple fact that she and her husband still loved each other. After what felt like a three-decade pause, the passion was back. It had never even occurred to Jules how bad the seemingly loveless marriage felt. Not finishing school all those years ago was beyond Jules' control. She was spinning so much those first few weeks and months after Sheila's death that she couldn't have gone back to school if she had wanted to. Jules knew that. She regretted it but partially accepted it.

On the other hand, her tepid relationship with Johnny was a mistake she felt she made every day by not doing anything about it. It was a marriage of death by a million cuts. Yet weirdly, plotting a presidential assassination with her husband brought the love back to their marriage. This realization made Jules giddy.

Enough with the trip down memory lane. Get up. Keep moving. Keep going.

She knew she had to keep practicing the shot, but she was feeling anxious. Her entire plan rested on her doing something she was sure she couldn't do. Johnny had told her that precision shooting is ten percent physical and ninety percent mental. She needed to relax, but how could she?

An hour later, she was on the Triumph, riding on the old country roads and feeling at peace. It was rebellious and dangerous and, above all else, fun. Maybe Johnny was right. They did need more fun in their lives!

APRIL 12, 1969

Jules was sitting alone in the front yard sipping lemonade.

Happy birthday to me.

She was about to go in when a brown Mercedes towing a small trailer pulled up. Seeing a car hitched to a trailer in the barracks wasn't unusual. People moved in and out all the time. Jules stayed put to catch a glimpse of her new neighbors.

When she saw Sheila's mom and dad get out of the Mercedes, she couldn't hide her joy.

"Oh my God!"

"Look at you!" said Sheila's mom as she went to hug Jules.

That hug felt so good, like a million hugs that had been missing had suddenly been replaced.

"So nice to see you, Jules," said Sheila's dad.

"You really do look great," said Mrs. Newman.

"Hope you don't mind us stopping by unannounced."

"Of course not."

"How many months are you now?" asked Mr. Newman, looking at Jules' large, pregnant belly.

"Seven."

"And how are you feeling?"

"Pretty good. Hardly any morning sickness. Some back pain, but mostly really good."

"Well, you wear it well, don't you?" said Mrs. Newman.

"How's Johnny doing?" asked Mr. Newman.

"He's okay. I got a letter from him two days ago, and he sounded good. Right now, he's in Saigon, which sounds pretty safe."

Jules was surprised how easily pretending to be the upbeat Navy wife came to her. Truthfully, she was always worried. It didn't help that Johnny's last letter differed from his previous ones. Despite news reports that combat was winding down, Johnny had hinted that things were about to get bad.

Despite this, Jules had learned from the other wives at the Navy housing at Mustin that putting up a good front was the job.

"From what I have been reading, the Tet Offensive was successful. Hopefully, all our boys will be home soon."

From your mouth to God's ears.

"Fingers crossed," said Jules before pivoting, "Can I get you two some lemonade?" She gestured to the small, mint green house behind her. She felt much more at home there than she ever had at her parents and was excited to show it to the Newmans.

"I wish we could, but unfortunately, we can't stay long. We're meeting the movers in New York and should get there before them to unlock the place."

"Of course," said Jules, disappointed.

She and Mrs. Newman had spoken on the phone a few days earlier, so Jules knew that the Newmans were moving, but she still felt a little sad that they wouldn't be close anymore. She decided not to dwell on that and instead be grateful that they stopped by.

Mrs. Newman put her arm on Jules' shoulder and held her eyes.

"But we couldn't leave Philadelphia without stopping by and seeing you."

"I'm so glad you did."

"And our place in New York has an extra bedroom, and you, Johnny, and your little one are always welcome," added Mr. Newman.

How are these two people still full of so much love and kindness after all they have been through? Even now, their humanity and grace shame anything my parents have ever shown me. This is what I've always needed—these two angels.

"We also want to give you a birthday present," said Mr. Newman.

They remembered!

Mr. Newman opened the trailer and rolled out Sheila's Triumph. Jules was speechless. That was it. All the tears came pouring out of her eyes.

Mrs. Newman hugged her once again, and this time, Jules hugged her back so tightly she wasn't sure she would ever be able to let go.

"Sheila would want you to have it. And we feel the same way," said Mr. Newman.

"I don't . . . I don't know what to say."

"We know you can't ride it right now, but after the baby, you should use it to get away. And trust me, there will be days when you will need to get away," said Mrs. Newman, wiping tears from her eyes.

Jules didn't think she deserved it. It should stay in Sheila's family. Surely, there must be someone else more deserving. She was about to say as much when she looked over and saw Mr. Newman's eyes water. Jules had never seen a grown man cry in her life. At that moment, she understood that the Newmans needed Jules to take the bike. They needed to get rid of it and know that Sheila's best friend was holding on to it. The least she could do was accept it.

Jules waved goodbye as they drove away. She stood in the same spot for almost an hour before wheeling the Triumph into her garage.

JANUARY 25, 2017

Jules was in the driveway, lying on Johnny's blanket in the snow, shooting at a Roma tomato can with his rifle—or, more aptly, trying and failing to shoot a can of Roma tomatoes. Every time she fired, she cringed with pain. After she looked through the scope and saw that she had missed by a mile, she cringed again with disappointment. As she reloaded, Johnny walked up behind her. She closed her eyes and smiled when he wrapped his arms around her. As gently as he could with a cast on, Johnny guided her finger to the trigger. Then he smiled, and they both laughed. She felt like they were in the pottery scene from *Ghost,* only with seventy-year-olds and a long gun.

She shot. Once again, she missed by a mile.

"Let me set it up for you," said Johnny.

She stood up to stretch while he aligned the scope, centered the rifle, and moved some dials. His movements were distinct and deliberate, but he was also visibly in pain with every twist and turn of his right hand.

Johnny looked back at Jules. "Come here."

She got back down on the ground, and he got on top of her.

"Now, take a deep breath."

She did.

"Do it again. This time, in through your nose and out through your mouth."

She did.

"Now, feel your breath in your lungs. Feel it expand and slowly leave your body. When it's gone, and you're one hundred percent empty, take a second ... good ... now, relax as you pull the trigger."

Jules closed her eyes and concentrated on her breathing. During a long exhale, she opened her eyes and, looking determined, she pulled the trigger.

She hit the pickup again.

"Goddamnit!"

They both stood up and looked at each other.

"At least you're consistent."

"Can we do this? Am I being crazy?"

"Yes. You're being crazy."

She laughed.

"But we still have twenty-four hours to work on it. You're still jerking your trigger finger just before you shoot. Let's keep trying," said Johnny.

CHAPTER 25

THAT NIGHT, WHILE JULES WAS in the kitchen cooking dinner, Johnny quietly set the dining room table. He dug through their big wooden hutch and found all the stuff they had been storing for half a decade: the old, lacey, white tablecloth that only came out on Thanksgiving, the china they had inherited from Johnny's parents, and a cherrywood box containing Jules' mother's silver. They had been gifted the flatware for their wedding, but they hadn't used it once in the almost fifty years of their marriage. Johnny polished two sets of silverware with a cloth, set them next to the china, and opened a 2012 Brunello di Montalcino Riserva. It was the only bottle of wine they had ever had that cost more than fifteen dollars; Richie had given it to them when he went to Italy two years earlier. Johnny dug out the 1920s Waterford Crystal glasses that they inherited from his grandmother when she died, which they had also never used.

When Jules yelled that dinner was ready, Johnny walked into the kitchen carrying two of his grandmother's Italian Blue Spode plates. He waved Jules aside, loaded the plates with the roasted chicken, Brussels sprouts, and mashed potatoes she had just cooked, and led her into the dining room.

"What's this?" asked a pleasantly surprised Jules.

"It's all the stuff we've been saving for a day that never seems to come."

Johnny set the plates on the table and pulled back a chair for Jules. "We deserve the best."

"Hell, yeah, we do," agreed Jules.

Johnny watched as Jules sat down, looked at the nice glass of wine, and pushed it to the side. His eyes widened when, instead, she reached for the water glass and moved it close to her plate.

Good for her. She seems determined to lay off the booze—more for me.

He picked up his wine and raised it for a toast. When she looked at her water glass worriedly, he assured her that any bad luck from toasting with water was already used up. He knew Jules was being respectful since he had always loved to bring up that superstition. It was a, as Jules would call it, "Navy thing." In fact, in the Navy, they often said that toasting with water or any non-alcoholic drink would cause a person to drown.

"No more bad luck for us."

Johnny loved making her smile.

As they enjoyed a romantic meal, they didn't talk about murder or Sheila. They didn't speak about Richie or Gina. But they also didn't sit in silence. Instead, they joked, told funny stories, and remembered good times from days gone by.

Right as Johnny sipped the last of his wine, there was a knock at the door.

"Now, who the hell is that?" said Jules.

Johnny went to the door and was greeted by Becca, Mia, and Jordan.

"Shit, it's the Breakfast Club," said Johnny.

Jules shushed him and pushed him out of the way to hug her granddaughter.

Jordan went to hug Johnny, but Johnny stepped back.

"What was that?" asked Johnny.

"I'm a hugger," said Jordan.

"I am not," said Johnny.

"Noted," said Jordan.

Sigh.

"And you're all here again because . . . why?" said Johnny.

"Oh, yeah. Bad news," said Jordan.

As Jordan rambled about Secret Service Agents coming in and out of the hotel all week, Johnny didn't know what he was getting at, but he did know that his romantic evening was over.

Jordan explained that the hotel manager, Steve, turned out to be a bit of an opportunist. When the Secret Service recommended sealing the laundry chute for security, Steve saw a chance to have the government pay for it. It made sense, since the hotel had service elevators and the chute was nothing more than an outdated money-suck in AC and heating costs.

"Well," said Johnny, holding up his cast, "I didn't think we were going to be able to go down there anyway."

Everyone looked at Jules. Who, in turn, looked at Johnny.

"I guess we could try to sneak down the stairs to the employees' entrance. But there are still many unknowns. What if someone in the stairwell recognizes us? Or a cop downstairs or on the street hears the shots, runs in, and sees us?" said Johnny.

"And that goddamn security cop," added Jules.

"Yeah, him. But, all that being said, this was never going to be easy," said Johnny.

"True dat. But that's not all," said Jordan.

Everyone turned to look at Jordan, who just sat there, nodding and smiling.

"And?!" said Jules.

"Oh, yeah . . ."

Jordan explained that Steve saw an opportunity to remodel the hotel. Johnny was about to inform Jordan that he could give a rat's ass about the hotel's aesthetic when Jordan mentioned that they had removed the lamps in all the rooms for space on the nightstands for a more modern coffee setup.

"Wait, are you kidding me right now?" said Johnny.

Jordan seemed surprised by Johnny's rage.

Jules looked at Johnny. "Oh, I'm so sorry. I know how much that rifle meant to you."

Forget what it meant. They would trace it quickly, and then Johnny and Jules would have a lot of explaining to do. Johnny fancied himself a good liar, but even he couldn't bullshit an explanation for why he hid a sniper rifle in a hotel across the street from where the President was speaking.

"We're all about to be in big trouble," was all Johnny said.

"Oh," said Jules, whose face turned white. "Perfect. We'll end up in jail, and we haven't even done anything yet."

There was a long, silent beat until Jordan remembered something and ran outside to his car. A few seconds later, he came back with the green lamp.

"I almost forgot; I grabbed your gun before they pulled the lamps out of your room."

"Seriously, you didn't think it was pertinent to start with that information?" said Johnny.

"No. But that's only because I don't know what 'pertinent' means. What is that?"

Johnny grabbed the lamp from the kid and considered smashing it over his head, but instead, he just walked away and returned to the dining room table. He could hear Jules saying goodnight to everyone as he folded himself onto his chair and stared at the mostly uneaten meal still on the table.

The best-laid schemes of mice and men.

A few days ago, Johnny would have been happy about the news. Outside forces putting the nail in the coffin of the whole endeavor was what he had been hoping for all along. But given everything that happened with Richie, he felt no joy seeing his wife deflated. In fact, sadness filled his belly.

Jules sat next to him. "Are we done?"

"I'm sorry."

"Me too."

CHAPTER 26

JANUARY 26, 2017

A SMALL GROUP GATHERED AT the Acorn Pub the following evening to celebrate Richie's life. When Johnny and Jules walked in, Johnny said that he was sick of memorials. The year before, they had been to three of them. Johnny commented, "We used to go to the movies, but now we just go to death parties. Getting old is overrated."

Jules laughed but disagreed. She remembered a full-on, new-agey professor who taught a "Death and Dying Interpersonal Psychology" class at college. She took it as an elective but ended up loving the class. On day one, the teacher walked into the room and said, "Hello. Let me start by saying that the best thing I can wish for all your young faces is that each of you has to deal with the deaths of many people you love." Jules was surprised that some of her classmates were taken aback by what Mr. Burns had said.

They didn't get it. They thought he was being rude, but it wasn't that. He was pointing out that experiencing the loss of many loved ones meant they had lived a long life and were loved by many. Grief and sadness were the only possible outcomes. If longevity and love were achieved, then the other part would be unavoidable. Jules found comfort in that idea.

The turnout for Richie's wake was staggering. The bar was filled wall-to-wall with people. Jules and Johnny made some small talk and heard sweet stories about how Richie never forgot anyone's birthday and never said no when asked for a favor. A church friend reminded Jules of Richie's dancing at a July Fourth clambake a few years earlier. The man loved to dance but had zero coordination.

After a half hour or so of reminiscing, Jules walked to the jukebox and played Lucinda Williams' "Passionate Kisses." Jules loved Lucinda but hadn't listened to her in years. Music was one of the many choices she had relinquished to her husband.

"Dance with me," she said to Johnny.

He smiled and raised his arms in a dancing position. Jules looked at Johnny and saw him in that moment as he had been when he was nineteen. He was in his dress whites, full of mischievousness and joy, and ready to show her a good time, undaunted by the burden of life. Jules closed her eyes, exhaled, and smiled from ear to ear.

They danced.

"You know Richie absolutely loved you?" said Johnny.

"I do. And he loved you too," said Jules.

They danced some more.

When the song ended, Johnny and Jules joined Ed and Linda, who were camped out on their regular stools. After they greeted one another, Johnny and Jules got drinks—a beer for him and soda water for her. Linda gestured to a sign above the bar that read: "Raise your glass to Richie Devlin," and said, "That's a good picture of him."

"Sure is," agreed Jules.

Ed raised his glass, "To Richie."

As they clinked their glasses, Linda turned to Jules, "How are you doing, dear? You seem down."

"For the love of God, we're at a wake. What? Should she be happy?" barked Ed.

"You know what I mean," Linda snapped back.

"It's been a rough few," said Jules.

It was silent. Then Johnny said, "It does baffle the mind that he dropped dead like that. Richie was the healthiest person I knew."

"Should have eaten more meat," said Ed.

What an ass. Ed never could understand why people loved Richie and loathed him so much. When you talked to Richie, he hung on to every word you said, whereas Ed never listened to anyone besides himself. The man loved the sound of his own voice. Richie was kind, loving, and gentle—three things Ed thought of as weaknesses. What an old, miserable piece of shit.

"Jesus," said Johnny.

"Give me a break."

"It just goes to show, though, you never know," said Linda.

"Amen to that," said Jules.

They all drank in silence for a moment. Ed took a big swig of his beer. "I am going to miss that pain in the ass. Although he was becoming a bit of an idiot the past few months."

Please shut up.

"Ed. Be nice," said Linda.

"No, I am. I'm just saying with all that doomsday crap about the election and all that hippie social justice nonsense, it sometimes felt like he forgot that he was white—"

Johnny was off his stool. Ed continued, "Sorry, you know what I'm talking about. I like—"

Before Ed could finish, Johnny punched him in the face and called him a racist piece of shit.

Two other guys pulled Johnny and Ed apart, but it was too late.

Jules stepped to the side and watched the ensuing old-people bar brawl. *Didn't have a bar fight on my Richie's wake bingo card. Somewhere, he must be smiling down on this and loving it.*

Twenty minutes later, Jules was driving their pick-up, and Johnny was in the passenger seat. His clothes were messed up, and he had a cut on his face, but he looked happy.

"I bet Ed will feel like crap tomorrow morning," said Jules.

"It was a good uppercut if I say so myself. I just wish I had done that years ago."

"Agreed."

Within an hour of getting home, Johnny was fast asleep. But Jules couldn't. Her mind was racing. She wasn't thinking about Richie, Ed, or Johnny. She was thinking "what-if?"

What if Sheila had lived? Would she and Johnny still be married? If Jules had gone to business school and gotten a New York City job, would Gina have even met Carl? If not, Becca would never have been born. Is that the point? Did Sheila need to die for Becca to be born? That was crazy thinking.

If she and Johnny had moved to New York after school, would Richie have been in their lives as much? How would that have affected his relationship with Kay? Would they have even met if it weren't for Jules?

And what about Sheila herself? What would she have been like if she had gotten old? Where would she live? How many kids and grandkids would she have had by then? Would she and Jules still be friends? Jules liked to think so, but she also knew that with time came change.

"What-ifs" were coming at her from every direction.

JANUARY 27, 2017

Jules looked at her phone, and it was 3:00 am. He would be in Philadelphia in a few hours. She had agreed to go to lunch in Lancaster with Johnny as a way to take their minds off what could have been. Why not? They both liked the buffet at the Shady Maple, so it would be a nice enough day. But Jules couldn't imagine being anywhere besides Philly. She needed to see him. One way or another, she needed it to be over.

JULY 1989

Fifty-three-year-old Jules walked out of the Broadway production of *A Few Good Men*. Johnny was a step behind her and grinning from ear to ear. She knew he loved the play, and she didn't hate it as much as she thought she would.

When they stepped into the lobby, camera flashes blinded them.

"What the hell is this all about?" asked Jules, referring to the gaggle of reporters.

"Who knows?" said Johnny.

When they got past the crowd, Jules turned to her husband. "That was the perfect anniversary present. Thank you."

"I knew you'd like it more than . . . what was the one you wanted to see?"

"Mandy Patinkin, *Dress Casual*."

"Yeah. Okay, I gotta hit the head. Meet you outside?"

"Sounds good," said Jules as Johnny rushed off.

Before Jules reached the exit doors, another camera flash went off. She turned to see what the hell was going on. Jules was shocked to see Sheila's rapist, his current wife, Mike Tyson, and Robin Givens leaving the theatre. She couldn't turn away as the Paparazzi surrounded the group of celebrities and he held court.

"How you doing, fellas? Doesn't my wife look great tonight!"

He twirled her around like a prop in his one-man show.

She looks bored.

"Do you want to comment on an article today in *The Daily News* saying that you're a thief ?"

"Rude. I want all New Yorkers to feel safe. Even the—"

He stopped mid-sentence when he spotted Jules across the room. It seemed he recognized her instantly.

Mike Tyson and Robin Givens waved goodbye and started to leave.

"Bye, champ," he said as he approached Jules.

"As I live and breathe, if it isn't Jules Dayitch."

"It's Jules Coletti. Has been for twenty years."

"Of course. And where is Mr. Coletti?"

"Johnny is in the bathroom."

Jules couldn't believe she was standing there talking with him and answering this man's questions. She wanted to run, to scream, to punch him, to do something, but Jules' reflex was to reset to polite conversation. Panic had somehow given way to social norms.

What the hell is that?!

He leaned in and whispered to Jules, "I still think about you. Sitting on your bed that day. The things I could have done with that bat."

Jules couldn't catch her breath.

"It's not too late for us. We can have a little thing on the side," he said before looking around to ensure that no one was close enough to hear him. He added, "I'd ask for your number, but you look slightly stressed. I'm sure I can find you if I need to."

He smiled and turned to the press, "Another fan. What can I say?"

The photographers snapped a few shots and followed him and his wife as they walked outside.

As he walked away, laughing, Jules stood there utterly gobsmacked for what felt like an eternity. She would probably have never left if Johnny hadn't eventually returned.

"Damn, the bathroom sink was leaking. I got water all over my shirt."

Johnny didn't even look up. If he had, he may have noticed that his wife looked terrorized. Instead, Jules turned and looked at the big wet spot on Johnny's button-down. The silliness of it snapped her out of her shock. "Oh, well. It's just water."

"Yeah."

CHAPTER 27

IN THE MORNING, JOHNNY WOKE up, felt the bruise on his face, smiled, and opened his eyes. *I bet Ed's face is worse!*

He turned to see if Jules was awake and was surprised that she wasn't even in bed.

Shit, where the hell is she?

Downstairs, he found his wife finishing the last of her coffee. He stood behind her as she gently placed the cup in the sink. He knew where she was going.

She screamed when she turned and saw Johnny standing there in his boxers and a white t-shirt.

"Mother of God!"

"Sorry. Didn't mean to startle you."

"Well, you did."

"I already apologized for that. And where the hell are you off to?"

"Goddamnit. I was trying not to wake you up."

"You failed."

"Let me go."

No.

"I need to be there today."

"So you can wallow in it? I told you we should stay as far away from there as humanly possible. Let's go to Shady Maple and get some sausages?"

Jules scowled.

Johnny knew she would not give in.

"Fine. If you have to be there, I will be there with you."

"Don't be a goddamn martyr."

"I'm not. We can watch the circus and stay in the hotel room over-night. Make a home vacation out of it."

"I think you mean 'staycation.'"

"Whatever-the-fuck. We can order more room service and see if we can capture lightning in a bottle twice in a row."

Jules smiled, "Sounds like a plan."

<hr>

Johnny had anticipated that the Marriott would be buzzing with activity, but it was genuinely overwhelming when he and Jules walked in. There were Secret Service agents, cops, reporters, and lots of looky-loos.

When a police dog started barking at Jules' suitcase, Johnny assumed they were cooked. Luckily, the dog's handler looked at Johnny and Jules and only saw two cute old people. The cop smiled and pulled the dog away from them.

But God forbid they have a moment to relax because, before Johnny could even squeeze out an exhale of relief, he saw Pags sitting in the corner on his stool and staring directly at them.

Johnny tapped Jules on her shoulder, and she turned around and saw what Johnny saw.

From what Johnny could tell, Pags had been using a coin to scratch an instant Bonus Cashword lottery ticket, but as soon as he looked up and spotted Johnny, he froze.

Johnny could see it click in the security guard's eyes as he con-nected the presence of Johnny and Jules, the police dog sniffing the suitcase, and the president being across the street.

Johnny watched the security guard's face fill with excitement. Undoubtedly, a retired cop would be eager to make his mark and get some attaboys from the brass. Stopping an assassination would be a big deal for anyone, especially an old guy likely put out to pasture.

When Pags stood up, Johnny already knew what was going to happen. He was going to come over and point his sausage fingers right in Johnny's face, and then the damn cop with the dog would be back, and within minutes they'd connect the dots. Johnny knew that his mulish wife couldn't let this go. He could tell from the weight of the suitcase in his hand and how the dog had sniffed at it that there was more than clothes and toiletries packed inside. That's why Jules was trying to sneak out before Johnny got up. And now they were both about to be thwarted by an imp of a man named Pags.

Goddamnit.

Just as Johnny had more or less given up and started to raise his hands in defeat, he noticed something had changed about the security guards' demeanor. His "gotcha" look morphed into one of shock and pure bliss. He was staring down at the ticket in his hand.

Johnny followed Pags' gaze, squinted, and made out three clown faces and a giant box with the word "BONUS" on the bottom of the ticket. Johnny played enough scratchers to know Lucky Circus rules. Johnny knew the piece of cardstock in the security guard's hand was worth a million dollars.

Pags looked up and smiled with a mouth full of teeth the color of candy corn.

Instead of approaching the would-be assassins, Pags took out his cell phone and ran outside.

Johnny just looked at Jules.

"What the hell was that?" asked a confused Jules.

"Lady luck," answered Johnny.

"What?"

"Who cares? Let's go," said Johnny.

Just when Johnny was about to enter the elevator, Jordan stepped out.

"What?! OH HEY! WOW!"

"Stay calm, you weirdo," said Johnny.

"Calm?! I am calm . . . But I thought you weren't coming anymore. I thought it was all, like, over?"

"Good morning, Jordan," said Jules.

"Um, where are your costumes?!" asked a nervous Jordan.

"Easy, Skippy. We're just here for some R and R," said Johnny.

"R, and what?"

"Sex. We're here to have hotel sex," said Jules.

Let that picture sit in your half-brain for a few Skippy.

Jules pulled her husband into the elevator. The doors closed.

Upstairs, post-sex, in his underwear and a t-shirt, Johnny sipped coffee and read the paper at the small desk. In front of him, Jules sat up in bed, eating a chocolate croissant.

Jules sang, "Sky rockets in flight, afternoon delight . . ."

Johnny laughed. "Would you stop?"

She kept singing, "Thinkin' of you's workin' up my appetite . . . Looking forward to a little afternoon delight . . ."

Johnny checked the time on his phone. *He should be here soon.*

He said to his wife, "Why don't I shower, and then we can head downstairs for a cocktail?"

Jules said nothing. She looked at Johnny, and the two made intense eye contact. There were no words. Johnny knew what was coming next.

CHAPTER 28

JULES SAT STARING AT JOHNNY.

He gets it.

Even though Jules knew her husband wanted to plead with her to listen to her better angels, he didn't say a word.

She watched as Johnny opened her luggage and found what he clearly knew would be there, his disassembled rifle.

"I thought when that dog started barking at our bag, I was screwed," said Jules.

"Old people's superpower."

"I guess we didn't need an oversized lamp after all. Once I took the parts out of the case and wrapped them in towels, they fit in here with no problem. I don't know why I didn't think of that earlier."

"Ah, well. You were taking precautions."

He started assembling the rifle, but Jules noticed he was struggling. She was in awe when he put the pieces on the bed and took out the Leatherman he always carried on his belt. He opened a perforated saw blade and hacked off his fiberglass cast.

I'm a lucky woman.

She smiled as he, once again, sans cast, started to assemble the rifle.

"Thank you," said Jules.

"You realize that twerp Jordan was right?" asked Johnny.

"How so?"

"When we walked in here, through the lobby, past the cameras, we were not in disguise," said Johnny.

"Yeah. That's why I didn't want you to come."

"Was never going to let you do this by yourself."

"I figured as much."

"And screw it. I can read some good books in prison," joked Johnny.

Jules didn't mind going to jail, but she did mind being locked up without even getting her chance.

Her chance at redemption.

Her chance at revenge.

Her chance at justice.

Jules didn't care which of those words was chosen to describe her motivation. She didn't care what the newspapers said or if she and Johnny got away with it. She didn't care about the optics, politics, news, or circus. She only cared about avenging her friend and being emotionally and mentally free of the Dummy's death grip.

"We're not getting caught. We're going to walk right out of here."

"And how do you suppose we're going to do that?" asked Johnny.

"I have a plan," answered Jules.

Johnny smiled.

Jules found the glass cutter she had ordered on Amazon in her bag and went to the window. She sliced a circle and pulled the glass inside using the device's suction cup.

"Quite frankly, I made a mistake trying to sneak out and do this without you. The afternooner relaxed me."

"I do what I can," said Johnny.

When the weapon was assembled, Johnny walked over to the window, cleared off the coffee table, and set up the detachable Harris 13" 1A2-LM bipod.

Relax, relax, relax.

Jules took long breaths as she watched Johnny attach the rifle and line up a shot for her.

"That's the best I can do," said Johnny, clutching his wrist.

"Does it hurt a lot?"

"Like you wouldn't believe."

She kissed him, then turned and looked out the window. "Should be any minute now."

Outside the Madison Hotel, Jules could see reporters, protesters, and fans crowded around the entrance, which was guarded by canine units, snipers, and undercover agents. Near the rear door, police caution tape and armed men kept crowds clear of the walkway leading to the ballroom entrance. All the dumpsters that had been lined up in front of the ramp leading to the ballroom entrance the week before had to be pushed to the side. A few had even been raised by hydraulic lifts. *Probably to guarantee a clean-looking, safe, photo-friendly entranceway.*

Jules stood at the window watching the spectacle.

Johnny said, "Once we get you set, we have to be quick. There are snipers on the roofs."

Jules smiled, walked over to the rifle, and got into position.

Johnny said, "Okay. Just remember—"

"Shush."

She put earplugs in, gently placed her hands on the rifle, and closed her eyes.

Inhale. Exhale. Inhale. Exhale.

With her one open eye, Jules saw that outside, the already frantic energy of the scene was rising further as a steady stream of cops on motorcycles pulled up in a synchronized parallel formation. Once the police officers were in place, more heavily armored motorcycles escorted black Escalades and specially configured limos. An agent exited each car, and, slowly, a sea of men in dark suits stood by the vehicle's doors. After some communication between the men on the ground and their superiors, it appeared the okay had been given, and suddenly, in an impressively synchronized motion, the back doors swung open.

From the rear of the motorcade, the President's oldest son shimmied out to cheering fans. He waved his hand at the people like a third-place beauty queen, and his smile quivered. Even through the thick windows, Jules could hear loud cheers for the former mayor of New York, who folded himself out of an Escalade and winked at the crowd with a full-on Nosferatu vibe. But the screams reached a Beatles-concert level when the President appeared out of the middle limo. Out of breath from just standing, he smiled an ugly smile, waved awkwardly, and moved completely gracelessly.

Inhale. Exhale. Hold it.

Jules slowly squeezed the trigger.

It took only one second, but it felt like an eternity. Her heart rate slowed, her breath hung in the air, and the red second hand on the wall clock froze.

Time stopped.

As the sound of the bullet leaving the gun filled the winter air, Jules watched—in what looked like slow motion—as reporters ran, spectators bellowed, and Secret Service agents and police drew weapons.

In the middle of all the pandemonium, a young aide dropped his briefcase as he dove back into one of the cars. The attaché popped open when it hit the ground, and a stack of papers flew in every direction.

The shot entered a pimple on the back of the White House's Chief Strategist. Before he fell to the ground, the bullet exited from some of that gross white stuff that had built up in the corner of his lip. From him, the bullet sailed into one of the former New York mayor's ears and out the other.

Next, the round flew in the president's direction and disappeared. Without hesitation, the Secret Service agents surrounded the President. Jules could read an agent's lips as he screamed, "Down! Down!" at the president and another agent yelled into a microphone on his wrist. The suited men in sunglasses then shoved him into a limo, and the car immediately peeled out.

GONE.

Jules watched his son scurry away from the scene and accidentally run smack into the hydraulic lift, which was hoisting a dumpster into the air. His knee bumped into the emergency release button, and the hydraulics gave way. The impact sent him backwards. He tripped and fell to the ground. After landing on his back, he looked up and saw the dumpster just before it fell right on top of him, squashing his insides out like a car running over a ketchup packet.

All around, the pages from the briefcase still rained upon the sidewalk.

One by one, people stepped on the discarded documents and ripped them to shreds. The very last thing Jules saw through the scope was a lone agent who spied her in the window on the third floor of the Marriott. He pointed at her and yelled, "Shooter! Shooter!"

The agent fired his Glock at Jules. Within seconds, dozens of agents took out their sidearms, and roof snipers trained their long rifles on the window. They all fired.

As the first bullet ripped through the Marriott's window, Jules let go of the weapon.

Something is pushing me. Jules could feel the weight of her husband thrust upon her as he tackled her to the ground. Countless more bullets shattered the window, and shards of glass fell like snow.

Johnny led the way. He pulled Jules with him as they army-crawled to the door. Once they made it out of the room and into the hallway, Jules sat against the wall, still shaking.

It happened so fast, but I think I saw them get him in the car.

"I don't know if I got him or not."

"Let's not worry about that right now. We have to get the hell out of—"

Johnny noticed that Jules' shoulder was bleeding. He examined the wound and saw that the bullet had entered right below her right clavicle and exited cleanly out the other side.

"You've been hit."

Jules looked down and saw the bleeding and just frowned.

Didn't even feel it.

"I don't think I got him."

"Jules! Focus!"

"It's okay. I can still walk."

Jules felt fine as Johnny helped her up and they walked a few steps. But suddenly, the pain became too much. She fell to the floor a few feet shy of the elevators. Johnny got her to sit up and lean against the wall.

What is happening?

The elevator and stairwell doors flew open simultaneously, and a dozen Secret Service agents flooded the hallway. The first agent stopped to check on Jules, and the rest ran down the hall.

"Are you okay, Ma'am?"

"It hurts like hell, but I'm okay," said Jules.

"Can you remember what happened?" the agent asked.

"My husband and I were in the hallway, returning to our room, but a man was there. And then there was a lot of shooting . . ."

Jules cut herself short and started fake crying. She could see Johnny rolling his eyes, but she knew the cops would buy it.

"There . . . were . . . so . . . many . . . gunshots . . ." said Jules.

When the agent looked up at Johnny, Johnny reached over to Jules and played along by comforting his wife.

"Did you get a good look at the man fleeing your room?" the agent asked.

"White guy. Beard. Late 30s, maybe early 40s. And I think he had sunglasses on. I think he went up toward the roof," bullshitted Johnny.

Good. Good.

The agent then spoke into his cuff-mic, "Suspect was seen heading to the roof. White male, early 40s, wearing sunglasses."

The thankful agent turned back to Jules and Johnny, "Thank you. EMS is right behind us. Hang on."

With that, he ran into the stairwell and presumably up to the roof. Seconds later, other agents followed him up the stairs. Slowly, Jules—with Johnny's help—stood up.

She winked at Johnny, "That's how I knew we'd get out. Like you always say, the only advantage of being old is that we're invisible to the rest of the world."

The elevator doors opened, and Jules passed out.

CHAPTER 29

ONCE AGAIN, JOHNNY AND JULES were in a hospital. Only this time, instead of a small town folksy one, they found themselves in a much more chaotic environment. But Johnny didn't care about the size of the hospital. He was just amazed that they were still free.

What is taking the cops so long to figure it out? They must have my rifle by now.

He looked at Jules, who was awake in bed, hooked up to an IV and several monitors.

What have we done?

Dr. Khan, a distinguished, older man, stood over her bed explaining how to clean and bandage her wound when she got home, but Jules didn't appear to be paying attention. She was looking at Johnny, who was sitting beside her bed, holding her hand. The two made prolonged, steady eye contact.

"All that to say, you're fortunate. The bullet went clean through your shoulder, and there doesn't appear to be any severe damage. Just a small flesh wound. Rest up, and we'll check in on you in a few," said Dr. Khan.

The second the doctor left, Jules turned to Johnny.

"I haven't had time to process everything that's happened, but it's starting to hit me that you stood by me. That is, I mean, you are something."

"Please, let's not go getting all sappy just as we're about to be arrested."

"Let me finish. It must not have been easy for you to come to the hotel, and you could have easily pried the rifle out of my hand in the room, but you didn't. Instead, you comforted and supported me throughout the chaos, and even now, when you have no idea what's coming next, you're here, still as a church mouse, just holding my hand, smiling at me. For a practical man, Johnny Coletti, giving yourself over to my plan was no easy task, but you did it."

"Well, what else was I gonna do?"

Johnny may have sounded glib, but he was thinking about what he had learned a long time ago, the same thing John Lennon had sung about after the Beatles broke up. The same thing that so many people realize in the wake of grief, pain, and trauma: even if "the dream is over," you can still believe in yourself and the people you love.

"Anyway . . ." said Jules as she got up out of bed. "It doesn't matter if I got him because he knows what he did. The pain of losing Sheila is still inside of me, and it will never go away. But I accept it now. I accept that she is gone." Jules ripped the IV from her arm.

"What the hell, Jules? Get back in that bed," said Johnny.

"Help me find my clothes and get changed. We have to get out of here before the cops show up."

"And where do we go? They'll get our address pretty damn fast."

"Don't worry. This was part of my plan."

"Getting shot was part of the plan?"

"No. And neither was coming to the hospital. But it can still work if we get out ASAP. The girls will be here any minute."

"The girls?!"

"Yeah. I texted Gina from the ambulance."

"What the hell?"

"Speaking of which, where is my cell?"

Johnny pointed to the bag underneath the bed, which contained her clothes and cell phone. Jules dressed and started pulling Johnny along with her out of the room and into the elevator.

In for a penny, in for a pound. I guess. But does she think we can get away from here and not be sitting in a jail cell by sundown? No way.

Downstairs, Jules hurried them to the exit. Johnny tagged along but came to a sudden stop in the waiting area. His eyes were fixed on the TVs, all of which were tuned to CNN. The sound was muted, but the crawl on the bottom of the screen read, "THE PRESIDENT OF THE UNITED STATES IS DEAD."

Johnny was speechless. *What the actual hell?*

"We have to keep going," said Jules.

"Look at the TV."

She stopped.

"What?"

She looked.

"We did it!" yelled Jules.

"Jesus. Keep it down."

Jules covered her mouth but couldn't hide her giant smile. Johnny was dazed.

"I thought you said you missed him," said Johnny.

"I don't know. I last saw him getting shoved into the car. I assumed I missed."

ONE HOUR AND FORTY-EIGHT MINUTES EARLIER.

Post-shooting, surrounded by agents, the President sat in the back of the limo, drinking a little bottle of water.

"That was unbelievable. What a bunch of sickos."

As he sipped the water, he noticed a small rip in his suit jacket and started pulling at it. A little blood leaked out.

THREE HOURS AND TWENTY-TWO MINUTES EARLIER.

On his way to the conference in Philadelphia, he was in his seat, devouring a K.F.C. chicken breast on Air Force One, when a Secret Service agent walked in and tried to hand him a Kevlar vest.

"I told you. I am not wearing that thing. It makes me look fat."

"But..."

He shooed the agent away and shoved more fried chicken into his mouth.

BACK TO ONE HOUR AND FORTY-NINE MINUTES EARLIER.

In the limo, he stared at the hole in his chest as blood spilled out like water from a leaky faucet. He seemed more curious than hurt and turned his attention out the window and said, "They forgot the coleslaw."

The President's heart then exploded.

Back at the hospital, Johnny felt his own heart stop. They were going to end up in prison—or dead.

Jules whispered to him, "Holy shit. I cannot believe it. Now we have to go. We have to disappear," said Jules.

The two ran to the front doors, but as they were about to slip outside, a woman jumped in front of them, "You two aren't going anywhere!"

Johnny took a step back from the sliding doors, looked up, and saw "little" Hallie Jackson blocking their escape.

What the living hell?!

"Goddamnit!" said Jules.

"What are you doing here?" asked a shocked Johnny.

"I do surgeries here on Wednesdays and am in the ER in Warrensburg the rest of the week."

"Wow. That's a hell of a schedule," said Jules.

"It's also a hell of a coincidence," said Johnny.

Dr. Jackson gestured to Jules' shoulder, which was bleeding through her shirt. "I don't know what you two are doing here, but I need to look at your wound before you leave."

"I'm okay," said Jules.

"Yeah, she's fine. It's not even her blood," lied Johnny.

"It's bleeding out of her body, so it had better be her blood, or I missed something important in med school."

Jules looked at Johnny, "You fancy yourself a good liar, huh?"

Fair.

Dr. Jackson examined Jules' shoulder, "This is a gunshot wound. What the hell is going on?"

Johnny stuck to the lie. "We were taking a small staycation. And this guy at the hotel we were at—"

But Jules simply said, "I shot the man who raped my best friend. I killed the President."

Johnny held his breath as Dr. Jackson stared at Jules. When she noticed what was playing on the TV behind them, Johnny knew it was all over. Instead, the doctor studied Jules' face for what felt like an eternity. She then smiled and walked away.

"Well, now we're done for. No doubt she's going to grab security," said Johnny.

"No way. She's cool," said Jules.

"What makes you say that?" asked Johnny.

"It's a woman thing," said Jules.

"Give me a break."

As they exited the hospital, Gina and Becca pulled up on the bike. Gina ran over to her mom and hugged her.

"Are you okay?"

"Fine. It barely scraped me."

Since when was Gina in on the plan? What were they doing at the hospital? Why is Becca driving the Triumph?

"Would someone tell me what the hell is going on?" said Johnny.

But before anyone could answer him, everyone else turned to look at Carl, who was walking up. "Hey, hey."

Jules looked into Gina's eyes. "I did it. I got him."

"I heard it on the radio."

They all hugged again, until Jules pulled away and wiped her eyes.

"Okay, Okay. Let's not get too sentimental." She gestured to the two cameras mounted above the entrance doors.

Johnny listened with disbelief as Jules said, "Those cameras need to show that you were dropping off our bike like I asked you to. As far as you know, I just wanted to drive home, and that's why Carl met you here with his car. No big deal. We'll all be having dinner tonight."

Becca hugged Johnny one more time.

"I love you, Pappi."

"I love you too," said a still baffled Johnny.

Jules hugged Carl.

Carl smiled, "You are one crazy old lady, and I will miss you."

Even Carl is in on this? Maybe I've been wrong about him all along.

Johnny felt Jules nudge him in the back, and when he turned, he saw that she was wearing a helmet and handing him the spare.

As he slipped it on, he heard her say to Carl, "Take care of our girls. And please help yourself to the frozen lasagna and meatballs in our freezer."

Gina hugged her mom. "I am so proud of you."

"Thank you. I love you."

There were more hugs and goodbyes, and eventually, Jules got on her Triumph and gestured for Johnny to get on behind her. When he did, Jules turned to her family on the sidewalk.

"I don't know how long it's going to be before we can reach out or if it's a good idea even to email or call you guys, but hopefully, it won't be too long, and there will be a way in the future to see you again. Hell, maybe you can visit us. So, this doesn't have to be goodbye forever. Just for now. Until we meet again."

"Until we meet again," said Carl.

"Until we meet again," said Gina.

"We'll see you soon, Grandma," said Becca.

"Where the fuck are we going?" asked Johnny.

"I'll explain when we get there," said Jules.

CHAPTER 30

JULES' MIND WAS CLEAR. SHE was at one with the road and the bike as she swerved along the country roads. Eventually, she turned onto the Pennsylvania Turnpike, then the Jersey Turnpike, and finally pulled into the long-term parking lot at Newark Airport.

Jules imagined that the FBI, Secret Service, and local cops were descending upon the hospital. She could picture lights and sirens, armored tactical vehicles, and helicopters.

She parked her bike and started to unpack their luggage.

"I still have a lot of questions," said Johnny.

He grabbed Jules by the shoulders, turned her around, and said, "What the hell is going on? Where are we going?"

Jules wiggled away from him, walked back to the saddle bag, and pulled out the blue duffel bag. She unzipped it, and Johnny saw that it was full of cash.

"We're going far, far, away from here."

Jules then imagined that the FBI, Secret Service, and local cops were descending upon their house. Again, she imagined lights and sirens, armored tactical vehicles, and helicopters.

"Jesus, Jules, what have you done? Where did you get all this money?"

"Don't worry. I didn't steal it, if that's what you're thinking. The first and only crime I've ever committed in my life was stealing from Wegmans, and the second was in that hotel room."

"Then where the hell did you get this?" Johnny asked, pointing at the bag full of cash.

"An angel," answered Jules.

"I swear to God. I will find the police myself and turn us both in. I'll beg them to throw me in the hole. Believe me, I could use the isolation right about now."

Relax, I'm trying to tell you.

"Do you remember on Thursday, the day after your cast was put on, we had the meatloaf, and Gina, Carl, and Becca came over?"

"I swear to—"

"Shush. Do you remember?"

"Yeah. I thought about that at Richie's service because it was the day before he died. We should have had him over. I don't know why I didn't call him that night—"

"Don't do that," interrupted Jules.

"Yeah," agreed Johnny.

"Anyway, it's funny that you should mention Richie because he's what I'm trying to tell you about. So that night, I was bummed. When the doctor said you couldn't use your arm, I felt it was all over."

"It was."

"Well, when you all went downstairs to play table tennis, I spilled my guts to Gina about everything. I went on about my mom and dad, my miscarriages, and then some."

"Why would you go into all that?"

Jules knew the real reason she had confessed was that she had had a few too many.

"Gina, of course, was already pissed that we were up to no good with Becca, and when I told her my plan, she thought I was crazy."

"She wasn't alone."

"Cute. Eventually, my babbling and confessing freaked her out enough that she went downstairs and left me alone. I was soaking the pots and pans in the kitchen sink when there was a knock on the window."

———

JANUARY 19, 2017 (*EIGHT DAYS EARLIER*)

Jules was still swimming in the shame of her confession to her daughter when she was startled by the tapping on the window. When she peered outside and saw Richie, she knew something was wrong.

"What the hell are you doing out there?"

"I was waiting to see you. I've been out here for almost an hour, waiting for Gina to leave. What the hell were you two talking about?"

Everything.

"Nothing."

"Could have fooled me. I thought it was never gonna end."

"Shush. You sound like Johnny. Are you hungry? I have potatoes and salad. And I think there's a Beyond Burger in the freezer I could heat up."

"Sorry, Jules. But I'm not hungry. I don't have much time because I want to talk to you before anyone else comes in here. So, forgive me for the bluntness, but I'm dying. I have stage-four pancreatic cancer."

What? No.

"I know, it sucks. I've known about it for a while now, and I think I don't have much longer."

What did he say? No way he just said he has cancer. Something's wrong. Maybe I do have dementia because there is no way.

"No."

"Yeah. That's exactly what I said when I found out. Anyway, I didn't tell anyone because I didn't want my last couple of days to be a pity party with false platitudes and bullshit. I just wanted to have some laughs and enjoy the people I love."

"Did you just say the last few *days*?" said Jules.

"I think so. I don't know. Days. Weeks. It doesn't fucking matter anymore."

No. No. No.

"Have you seen specialists? You know, Johnny's old boss saw this renowned oncologist at Sloan Kettering in New York. I'm sure he could put you two in touch," said Jules.

"See, crap like that, that's exactly why I didn't tell anyone; I don't want to do this right now. I don't want to have those conversations. Trust me. I've seen everyone I need to see. It is what it is, and nobody can do a thing about it. I'm a dead man walking, which is why I'm here now. I can feel it, Jules. It won't be long."

Richie then darted back outside, where he picked up a blue duffle bag—the same one that Gina had handed to Jules at the hospital. He dropped it on Jules' kitchen table.

Okay, stop. This is ridiculous. I need to think. We can fix this.

"It's everything I have, minus fifteen thousand I needed for something else. But there's about five hundred thousand in there. When I found out I was sick, I did one of those reverse mortgages they always advertise on the news. I also sold a bunch of shit, including some stock. This is pretty much all of it right here. I want to give it to you and Johnny to help you take down the monster. What he did to Sheila all those years ago was disgusting, and God knows how many other women along the way. He's capable of destroying everything, and I want to help you guys end him. I know Johnny is still on the fence, but half a million can go a long way to change people's minds. Plus, I know you better than you know yourself, Jules Dayitch. And you're not going to let this go. So do what you want with this cash. I leave it to your discretion."

He called her by her maiden name—the sweetness. Jules pushed the bag to the side, reached out, and held Richie's hands. They smiled at one another and were still and quiet for a few minutes.

Then, Richie said, "Now. If you have any rainbow cookies hidden around here, I will take one of those."

Perfect. Jules got up and grabbed a Tupperware full of the Italian pastries from the top shelf of a cabinet by the stove and handed it to her friend.

They talked some more and ate cookies. He cried, she cried, and they hugged.

———

JANUARY 27, 2017

In the airport parking lot, Johnny was speechless.

"I'm sorry I didn't tell you, but that's what he wanted," said Jules.

"Jesus, he died the next day. So, he did know."

"I will say I have never in my life seen a man so at peace with death. He was ready," said Jules.

"The strength," said Johnny.

The kindness.

"Cancer like that lays out the strongest of men. But not that ox. He was walking around, lugging bags of cash. Shit, he painted all that stuff in his garage and put the deer stand up in the tree. I mean, he was joking and carrying on in the bar right until he dropped."

Johnny lowered his head, and Jules put her hand on his cheek. Poor Johnny. How hard it must be never to allow yourself to cry, to be told from a young age to hide your feelings and keep your love hidden, to have the tenderness beaten out of you as a boy, and then witness so much death.

She held her hand on his face for a few more seconds.

"Once I had the money, I knew we had a real chance if I could come up with an escape plan. That is where I was stuck: number nine of my ten-point plan. I knew that with your military record, our DNA in the hotel room, and all the CCTV footage, even if we were in costumes, it wouldn't take them long to know it was us. We couldn't get away with it since they would know we pulled the trigger. The only option was to disappear. Like Richie said to me when I first told him about the scheme, it wasn't about getting away with it. It was about getting away from it. And since it was guaranteed that they would know our identities by now, the only way to get away was to become other people. But how do we do that?"

"Good question," said a confused Johnny.

"Well, the morning after Richie gave me the money, while you were at Wawa playing numbers, Gina came over."

"Jesus Christ. This is starting to sound like *A Christmas Carol*, with you being visited by three ghosts."

"Yeah, and you're the Scrooge. Now, shush and listen. Early that Friday morning, I was outside chopping wood. Even though there was more than enough inside already, I couldn't just sit and watch the news. I needed to do something physical."

JANUARY 20, 2017 (*SEVEN DAYS EARLIER*)

After Jules felt the pain of splitting the logs and had her "now what?" epiphany, Gina's Jeep rolled up the driveway. Jules got up and watched as her daughter got out and walked to her.

"What are you doing here so late? Is Becca okay?"

"Everyone is fine."

Okay, then, what is it? Are you here to have me locked up in a loony bin? Get to it. I don't have time for this right now.

"Did you watch the inauguration this morning?"

"I couldn't."

"Well, I wish I hadn't. And just so you know, Carl and I talked this morning and decided to meet at our lawyer's after he got off work."

"What for?"

"To move you and Dad to an assisted living facility."

"Oh, here we go again."

Jules started to stack the wood she had chopped.

"Just listen, Mom. Carl and I talked about it, and we made our decision. And last night, when you told me about what you wanted to do, I was even more convinced that you needed help, but—"

Gina paused. Jules stopped stacking wood and moved closer to her daughter.

"I was really upset last night, and when I woke up this morning, I called in sick. Mental health day, I told them. By 8:00 am, Becca had slunk downstairs and headed off to school, leaving me alone. Being alone in our house is weird for me. Like, I didn't know what to do. So, I went online and researched dementia, delusions of grandeur, and paranoid schizophrenia. But the internet is so depressing. I gave up, made more coffee, inhaled a piece of coffee cake, folded myself onto the couch, and dove into the TV. When the inauguration coverage began on CNN, I couldn't turn away. I could not believe it was happening. But it was. For weeks, like so many people, I just assumed somebody would do something, or some greater force in the government or the world would stop it from happening. But nobody's coming. Nobody's doing anything. It's real; worse, this will be the world my daughter will grow up in."

"I can't," replied Jules.

"That's why I drove over here."

"Why?"

"I want to help you."

"Help me with what?"

"I want to help you kill him."

CHAPTER 31

JOHNNY LISTENED TO JULES EXPLAIN their daughter's rationale. He was astonished.

"She apologized for getting mad and was empathetic and understanding about what I was trying to do. She told me stories about some of those awful men she dated before Carl."

Don't get me started on those idiots.

"Do you remember Doug?"

"I hated that guy," said Johnny.

"We both did. It turns out we were right to hate him because Gina told me that Doug once slipped something in her drink. It wasn't even at a bar or party. It was at Gina's apartment when she, Doug, Beth, and her boyfriend, Bruce, were watching movies. Luckily, Beth saw him do it, and she and Bruce kicked Doug out. After that, Gina stayed away from that asshole."

"Jesus." Johnny felt himself filling with rage.

"Right? I won't go into it all, but suffice it to say that Gina has had more than a few close encounters with creeps. Anyway, after she told me all of this, she said she wanted to help get the asshole. I, of course, told her no way and that I didn't want Becca to get involved. But she insisted and had a plan for us to disappear. Number nine of my ten-point plan was her idea!"

Enough with the ten-point plan already.

"She said we should steal Ed and Linda's passports."

"Oh, Jesus Christ."

"I know, I thought it was dumb, but then Gina explained her logic. Ed and Linda weren't planning any trips anytime soon, so they wouldn't notice they were missing for months if not years."

"But we look nothing like them," said Johnny.

"You're such a contrarian. I know we don't look like them, but it doesn't matter. You say it all the time. It's old people's superpower; we're invisible to the rest of the world. Nobody is going to scrutinize our IDs because, to them, we're just cute, soft, cuddly oldies—ghosts."

Johnny shrugged, "True."

"The only thing we weren't sure about was how to get the passports. Now, I do have a spare key, but I wasn't sure when Ed and Linda would be out of the house long enough. Gina had this crazy idea that I could invite Linda out for drinks while you and Ed were at the pub, but when I called Linda that day, she said she didn't feel well and was staying in."

"Can you please cut to the chase? I have to pee."

"Yeah. Me too. So, we were still working out a time to get them, and then—"

"Richie died. That's why Gina wasn't at Richie's service."

"Yeah. We knew Ed and Linda would be out of the house, so Gina snuck over there. She was already wearing black clothes and only needed to slip on gloves and a ski mask. She used my spare key to go in and went upstairs into Ed and Linda's bedroom, where she found the lockbox. Linda's got a big mouth, so I knew their lockbox key was on the nightstand, so it was all pretty easy. Once Gina had the passports, she put everything back, locked up, and voilà."

Jules reached into her pocket and produced the two passports.

"So, you lied. Today wasn't your second crime. It was your third."

"No. It was. Gina broke in, not me."

"Sure, but you could still be arrested for aiding and abetting, and I imagine aiding and abetting the theft of a passport is a federal offense."

"Whatever. I just killed the President of the United States. Are you ready to take a trip?"

Johnny had a thousand thoughts and questions but let them all go. Instead, he held her hand and walked toward the airport.

Inside, they peed, checked the bag of cash, and had some lunch.

An hour later, at the gate, Johnny was actually feeling excited. *My crazy wife may have pulled this off. Amazing!*

Jules pulled out the stolen passports, and the thirty-something customs agent didn't look twice. *If you've seen one old person, you've seen them all.*

They boarded, stowed their luggage, and took their seats in first class. He ordered champagne. She got sparkling water. They clinked glasses, and the plane took off.

CHAPTER 31

FEBRUARY 2017

ED SAT IN HIS LIVING room, eating dinner in front of the TV just like he had every night since the incident. He was still reeling from the news that Johnny and Jules had assassinated the President.

"Plus, that son of a bitch never paid me the five hundred dollars."

Outside, the Suburban's bumper still had the bullet hole in it.

Both Ed and Linda had become obsessed with trying to make sense of it. Especially mind-boggling to Linda was how they got away from the cops. If she had looked in her lockbox and noticed their passports were missing, she might have been able to put the pieces together and help the authorities. Instead, she wouldn't notice for more than a year.

Pags and his wife sat in a luxury VQ45 sports cruiser on Greenwood Lake in New Jersey and fished. Neither one of them had a care in the world.

Warrensburg High School received an anonymous gift of fifteen thousand dollars. The money was donated with the stipulation that it must be used to reinstate the Debate Club. They did, and the Boston trip was back on. Becca had a great debate, and Warrensburg won.

Meanwhile, 7,647 miles away in the Serengeti, Tanzania, at the magic hour, Jules and Johnny were on her dream trip.

Jules watched as Johnny once again looked through crosshairs, only this time with a new Canon 5D Mark IV camera. He was snapping shots of a lioness—the primary hunter in any pride—as it killed a water buffalo. She was so happy to see him taking photos again. It had been too long, and he was so good. She closed her eyes and felt the same way she had felt all those years ago when a shy, weird, teenage boy had first shown an overzealous teenage girl his soul.

As Johnny snapped the shot, he caught Jules looking at him. He turned and smiled. There she was. The Jules he had almost forgotten existed.

She did it. She changed the world.

Everything was going to be okay.

ACKNOWLEDGMENTS

I AM A LUCKY MAN. My mother not only inspired Jules into existence but also encouraged me more than anyone to get this story out into the world; she is my hero. And my father, despite having ideological differences with the story, read many drafts and offered unwavering support—thank you, I love you both.

I couldn't have done this without the editing of Sangeeta Mehta and Kayla Kauffman, as well as the literary expertise of David Wogahn. I would also like to express my gratitude to Dan Hood for his insightful—and often hilarious—notes.

Finally, I want to thank Jean and Bruce for their support. They are the two easiest people to love and the only reason I get out of bed in the morning. XXOO.

ABOUT THE AUTHOR

The Triumph of Jules Coletti is Brian Finkelstein's debut novel, but storytelling has been his life's work for more than twenty years. His solo shows have packed theaters, his story *Perfect Moments* was featured in *The Moth*'s landmark collection *50 True Stories*, and his television writing has earned him two Emmy nominations. He's also sold screenplays and written comic books.

On stage, Brian has performed everywhere from the HBO/U.S. Comedy Arts Festival in Aspen to the Summer Nights Festival in Perth, Australia. A longtime host and storyteller with *The Moth*, his tales have been heard worldwide on public radio shows including *Good Food*, *The Business*, and *Marketplace*.

www.ingramcontent.com/pod-product-compliance
Lightning Source LLC
Chambersburg PA
CBHW050836180626

46814CB00007B/2483